Laura D. Bastian

ECHOES OF Summer

a novel

Lange House Press

Lange House Press

Other Books by
Laura D. Bastian

Sink or Swim
Eye on Orion
Beyond Orion
Heart of Orion
Guardians of the Gate

Cover Design by Novak Illustrations
Edited by Paula Buckendorf
Interior Design by Lange House Press

ISBN-10: 1944137009
ISBN-13: 978-1-944137-00-7

Chapter One

Madison peeled the wrapper off her fun-sized Butterfinger and popped it in her mouth. She rarely indulged, leaving the candies on her desk for clients, but she'd worked through lunch on a presentation and was starving. Only seventy-three minutes until she was off and could head home. She'd swing by Jessie's Grill and get a juicy burger and a huge order of cheese fries and some plain ones for Milo. Her seven-year-old thought the only good thing on a fry was ketchup.

She took a drink of water and swished her mouth out then took a breath mint before her appointment with her boss. She grabbed her laptop, wondering if he wanted to see the proposals for snagging the Doewin's company she'd been working on with Robert for the last few weeks. If they could nab that new personal hygiene manufacturer, it would skyrocket Carlson Ad

Agency to the top.

A quick glance at her clock told her it was time to head to Mr. Carlson's office. She opened the glass door and fitted her smile into place. First impressions happened more than once, no matter what it was called. Every time you saw or heard of a person or product, a new opinion formed. That's why she went by her middle name instead of Beatrice. Madison sounded much more professional, yet still fun and interesting. Not old lady. It was always a good idea to show her best, and a smile was the place to start.

"Great work on the cereal account, Madison," Robert said as he joined her in the hallway on his way to his office.

"Thanks, Robert. I hear you've almost closed the deal with the sports drink. You've got this." Madison gave him a thumbs up, and Robert returned it half-heartedly before disappearing through his door. He'd been struggling lately to stay focused with his daughter fighting leukemia. Madison had been filling in for him on the Doewin's proposal and was close to being ready.

Madison smiled and nodded at the others in the office as she made her way to Mr. Carlson's door.

His secretary smiled and waved her in. "He's expecting you."

"Thanks, Kathryn. I love your necklace. Was that something from your trip?"

Kathryn's eyes lit up. "Yes, my husband picked it out at this cute little shop we'd stopped at after touring the lava tubes. Oh, I wish I could go to Hawaii once a month."

Madison smiled. "Wouldn't that be fun? I'm so glad you got to go." Hawaii was on her bucket list. As long as she didn't visit *his* island, she'd be fine. Maybe once she closed this latest deal, she would go, but she didn't really want to go to Hawaii with a young child alone, and there was no one in her life at the moment who could accompany her.

The secretary rubbed the plumeria flower design between her fingers with a dreamy look on her face.

Madison sighed. "You'll have to tell me all about it soon. Tell Trisha hi for me, will ya?"

Kathryn nodded. "Will do." She returned her attention to the computer monitor, and Madison reached for the door to Howard Carlson's office, thinking about the guy she swore she'd never waste another minute on. Stupid Hawaii. Stupid Hawaiian family who sent their drop-dead gorgeous son to work his grandpa's farm every summer since he was fourteen. Stupid first kiss that had melted her soul and then turned her into an idiot with every one of his kisses that followed. She hated thinking of Stephen, but every time she looked into her son's eyes, she could see his father clearly.

Madison forced the memory of Stephen Kohalohini back into the box he'd been breaking out of for the past eight years and opened the door. Mr. Carlson stood as she entered, and a man with broad shoulders, shiny black hair, and beautiful brown skin stood and turned toward the door.

Her mouth dropped open to see the very man she'd just banished from her thoughts standing in front of her. He smiled, showing perfect white teeth against his full lips, and that familiar crinkle that surrounded his eyes reminded her of all the good times they'd shared over that summer. Of the mischief they'd gotten into. Of the only time she'd been arrested.

"Madison," Mr. Carlson said, waving her closer. "I'd like you to meet Stephen Kohalohini." Mr. Carlson looked at Stephen as if asking if he'd pronounced the name right.

Stephen smiled, "You're a natural, Mr. Carlson."

"Stephen, this is Madison Perry, the best account executive we've ever had."

Madison froze a few feet away from the desk and stared at the dark brown eyes studying her. He didn't remember her. She'd gone from chestnut to blond, learned how to use makeup, went by her middle name for work, and had gained twenty pounds, but apparently she'd been so forgettable Stephen didn't remember those summers together at all.

4

Mr. Carlson took a few steps around his desk and stood next to Madison. "I'd like you to show Stephen around the office. I've hired him as a consultant to help us increase our productivity and get some more clients. He'll also help you cover for Robert as new client manager until Robert gets back into full swing." Mr. Carlson looked at Stephen. "I'm excited to have you with us."

"I'm excited to be here as well, Mr. Carlson. And Madison, I've heard so much about you. It will be a pleasure learning the ins and outs of this office from you." Stephen extended his hand, and Madison forced the smile to return to her lips. First impressions and all that. The second his long fingers wrapped themselves around her small hand her heart fluttered, and she knew she was in trouble.

Stupid heart.

Stephen couldn't believe his luck. He'd be working closely with this blond-headed beauty. If he understood right, this was the little lady he'd be working with on the Doewin's account. Mr. Carlson wanted that deal. He was sure he could help bring this agency into the twenty-first century and get them utilizing social media and Internet options for advertising.

Madison's smile captivated him, and something about it seemed familiar, but he couldn't place it. Not many women left a lasting impression on him, but Madison was well on her way to it. In fact, the more he looked at her, the more he felt he knew her from somewhere.

Madison turned to Mr. Carlson, and Stephen felt the loss of her hand as she pulled back from the handshake he hadn't released yet. He wanted to look into her hazel eyes and see that smile turned back to him but focused on the words Mr. Carlson said.

"Stephen will be a wonderful resource to work with. I'd like the two of you to collaborate on the Doewin's pitch. He can give you some pointers on how to catch the new crowd."

Madison's smile slipped, and her face whipped around to study Stephen. The daggers in her gaze surprised him, and his own smile dropped away. Was this the first she knew about their working together? Madison turned back to Mr. Carlson and stammered for a moment before taking a quick breath and starting over.

"I am sure Mr. Kohalohini is a wonderful consultant, but I don't think I need his help on this." Stephen was surprised she hadn't butchered his name

6

like most mainlanders did. "Robert and I have some really good ideas. Besides, what will Doewin think about switching from Robert this far into the negotiations? I don't think it's the best thing for us to do at this time."

"Nonsense," Mr. Carlson said. "Things like this happen all the time, and you are still involved. In fact, I don't think Robert has spent more than a few hours with any of the representatives from Doewin. You've been our face. Stephen here will slip into position easily, give you pointers, and help you hook them deep, and reel them in. Besides, Robert has requested time off to spend more time with his family. When things improve with his daughter, we'll bring him back in and you can share what you've learned from Stephen." He patted Madison on the shoulder.

Madison nodded slowly as if coming to terms with the changes, but she didn't look pleased. Mr. Carlson turned to Stephen. "I expect a detailed proposal from you tomorrow morning first thing. Doewin is being courted by too many agencies. I want them signed with us soon."

Stephen nodded. "We'll get them." He turned his gaze to Madison. "I've got some great ideas and would love to hear what you've got as well."

"Have her explain them over dinner," Mr. Carlson said. "You can count it as business expenses and get her out of the office. She spends too much time in here as it is."

Madison stared at Mr. Carlson as if she couldn't believe what he'd just said, but Stephen wasn't going to argue. Especially when just given permission to take this lovely woman out to dinner. Madison couldn't turn him down for dinner without upsetting the boss, and he was going to make sure he took advantage of this opportunity to impress the heck out of her.

Stephen thanked Mr. Carlson and ushered Madison toward the door. "So tell me what you've got so far. I understand you've been working on this proposal for quite some time." Stephen glanced back at Mr. Carlson who had returned to his desk chair and picked up his phone exuding the attitude of *don't interrupt me*.

The second they got out the door, Madison smiled at the secretary who nodded sweetly in return and waved a couple fingers as she talked to the person on the other end of the phone. It was obvious Madison was well-liked in the office, and her open personality would help them land this account. She dropped the smile the moment she caught sight of him, making him second-guess his assessment of her qualities. She marched down the hallway, and Stephen had to take huge strides to catch up.

"Should we save the tour of the office until

tomorrow, and we can get started on the proposal right away?" Stephen asked.

Madison slowed down a fraction and pointed stiffly with one hand. "The copy room and supply closet is over there. The breakroom is over there. The restrooms are behind you down this hall. And I have no clue where your office is."

Stephen blinked in surprise at her tone but tried to ignore it. "No worries, I'll just follow you to your office where we can get to work. Then we can head right to dinner." He pulled out his phone and instructed the voice-activated assistance to find the phone number to his favorite restaurant.

Madison stopped and whirled around. "I'm not going to dinner with you. You can order take-out if needed, but we'll be here in the office until seven. Then I'm leaving. I have a prior commitment."

Stephen shut off his phone and nodded. "Chinese… or pizza?"

Madison blinked, and a strange expression crossed her face. It reminded him of something, but she shook her head and said, "Pizza. Deep dish. Chicago-style." She spun on her heels and marched forward, giving him a view of her long hair that reached the center of her back, her healthy curves below that, and strong calves leading to her fitted knee-length skirt before she disappeared into what he assumed was her office.

Oh, he would enjoy working here with someone of her spunk and personality.

Chapter Two

"Unbelievable," Madison muttered as she let the door to her office swing shut behind her. She texted her sister to see if Milo could stay until seven and sighed with relief when she said no problem. Her eyes fell on the picture of her son on the corner of her desk. He should have had a daddy who cared, but instead Milo had gotten a man who'd never even returned her phone calls or emails and didn't know he existed. Madison opened her laptop and grabbed a Butterfinger while her mind wandered to her first sight of Stephen in Mr. Carlson's office. As her mind flooded with images of his broad shoulders, she shook her head. "The jerk doesn't even remember me, and here I am thinking about how much he's filled out over the years." She grabbed another candy, ripping the wrapper off and shoving it in her mouth followed soon by a third. She needed to get a grip. She was better than this, and she'd never acted so rudely to a co-worker in her life.

But she'd never had a bad break up with someone she was expected to work with either.

How could Mr. Carlson do this? Hire someone to teach her about Internet marketing? She'd been trying to convince Mr. Carlson for ages to branch out, yet he always wanted to stay with his tried and true. Now he was hiring a man to do what she already knew. And why hadn't Robert mentioned something about this? She'd been working on this project with him for weeks and he'd never once mentioned he was considering taking time off.

A knock on her door made her jump. She grabbed the picture of her son and slid it into the drawer, then chewed fast, shoving the candy to one side of her cheek. "It's open."

Stephen popped his head in her office. "Mind if I come in?"

Madison took a slow breath before responding around the chocolate still in her mouth. "Of course not. Have a seat." She pointed to the chair her clients usually occupied, and she walked around the desk slowly to give herself time to swallow. She took a sip of her water bottle and adjusted her smile into place.

Stephen's deep brown eyes studied hers, and she felt uncomfortable. He probably could tell she didn't want to work with him. She needed to be more professional than that.

"Look, Madison," Stephen began, "I wanted to apologize if I sounded forward back there. I should have consulted you first on whether you had plans for the evening. It was wrong of me to assume you were willing to go to dinner just because Mr. Carlson suggested it. I think you're right that staying here in the office is a better idea. We have all the resources we need to pull together a fantastic proposal and still get you to your appointment in plenty of time."

Madison smiled at his use of the word appointment. He almost seemed to be asking for more details. Well, let him think she had a date. "Apology accepted. And welcome to the company. Before we get started on the proposal, do you mind sharing with me some of your prior experience?" She wanted to know about his past and where he'd been for the last eight years, but that would have been totally inappropriate to ask.

Stephen leaned back into the chair and lifted one foot onto his knee, looking completely at ease in her office.

She kept her back straight and put on her most professional smile as she listened to him describe his education all the way back to his high school on Oahu then his university training in southern California during the same time she'd been giving birth to and raising his child alone. He moved onto the different ad agencies where he'd worked, some of which surprised her. He was talented, and when he described some of the accounts he'd been involved in, Madison understood why Mr. Carlson was so excited to have him at their agency.

That didn't mean she had to be happy about him being there, but if she wanted to keep her job she would have to be careful how she acted. And since he didn't remember her, she would let it stay that way and keep Milo completely out of this. Besides, Stephen likely wouldn't be here long. Robert would return; there was no way Mr. Carlson would replace his stepson permanently.

When he finished, Madison nodded, impressed. "I'm glad you've joined us then, Mr. Kohalohini." She opened her laptop and found the files she'd been working on, feeling nervous to show him her work. What if he wasn't as impressed? She turned the laptop around and slid it across the desk toward him but kept her hands on the back of it to indicate she didn't want him to just take it.

Stephen took the hint and moved his chair closer to the desk. He flipped through the images and nodded at a few, zoomed in closer at a couple, tilted his head at some to get a different angle, and passed it back.

"Nice. I think you're on the right track."

Madison pulled her laptop back and turned it to herself, contemplating his words. *Right track.* What exactly did he mean by that? His voice was deep and warm, just like his eyes, and it hadn't sounded condescending at all, but it wasn't a glowing compliment either.

"Do you have a note pad and pencil I could use? I didn't bring my laptop today." Stephen glanced at her desk and at the bookshelf she used mostly as decoration.

Madison pulled open the drawer just above her lap and passed him a pencil she was surprised to find in there. She hesitated for a second, then turned around and grabbed a sheet of paper from the printer.

Stephen smiled and took it from her hand, brushing her fingertip with his — completely unnecessarily since the paper was a standard eight-and-a-half by eleven, and she'd handed it to him the long way. Madison pulled her hand back and wondered awkwardly what to do with it. Part of her wanted to tuck it behind her back and rub the sensation off on the fabric of her skirt; the other part of her wanted to caress that spot with her opposite hand to see if anything was different, and why his touch still affected her so much.

She did neither and instead adjusted her chair

before sitting down again. As Stephen began jotting down notes to himself he suggested some ideas and how they could incorporate her ideas in a way that would impress Doewin the most. He elaborated on a few of her ideas to take to the Internet, suggesting the same things she had thought of doing, yet hesitated on because Robert didn't want to go that direction.

At first, Madison wondered if he would take all her ideas and change them, but as he laid out a plan as to which ideas had the most merit and which ones could be used to pitch potential commercials and ad spots for radio, television, magazines, and social media sites, Madison knew they had a better chance at landing Doewin with Stephen's help.

And that annoyed her to no end.

Stephen had helped himself to a few more papers from her printer and continued scribbling things to himself, sharing a couple ideas on occasion. Madison took the sane approach, opened a document on her laptop, and made notes of what they discussed. She'd need it on there anyway for when they presented the plan to Mr. Carlson.

A knock on her office door was followed by Robert's head popping in. "Do you have a second? I just saw Howard—" He caught sight of Stephen, and his demeanor changed immediately. He stood straighter and squared his shoulders as he entered the room and moved over to Stephen with his hand out. "I'm Robert Noyes."

Stephen put his pencil down and stood up to shake Robert's hand. "Stephen Kohalohini. It's a pleasure to meet you, Robert. I'm sorry to hear about your daughter."

Robert's eyes turned sad. "Thank you."

Stephen led Robert over to a chair and began asking him about how things were going, if he had any suggestions on what to do with the Doewin's proposal so they could add them, and talked about how much time would be freed up for Robert to spend time with his family.

Robert's postured relaxed. "Howard's a good man. It will be good to be home more to support Melissa and the kids." He turned to Madison. "I'm sorry I didn't give you any warning about this change. There's just been so much on my mind lately."

Madison shook her head. "Don't worry about it, Robert. You need to do what's best for you and your family. I hope you'll be back with us soon."

Robert nodded and got up to leave. "Thanks for all the help you've been on these projects. I couldn't have made it this long without you." He walked out the door, and Madison turned to find Stephen studying her.

A knock on the office door announcing the pizza

delivery saved her from speaking to Stephen.

Stephen paid him with cash and didn't keep the receipt to turn in for work expenses, and Madison wondered if he had ulterior motives. She pushed the idea out of her mind. He didn't even remember her, so he wouldn't be trying to impress her or anything. She wished she could forget him as easily.

But now he was in front of her in the flesh, and that flesh was so fine he put every memory of his teenage self to shame. She turned away, hoping to gain some control over herself if she was going to be forced to work with this man. At least it would only be temporary. She prayed Robert's daughter would get better soon so he could be back to get the training from Stephen. She needed to stay far away from Stephen, and working with him made that impossible.

She pulled out a slice of pizza and sat on the edge of her desk to look at the notes on Stephen's papers but couldn't understand what any of it meant. She took a bite and sighed at the taste. So much better than a handful of mini candy bars.

Stephen stopped short before the slice of pizza reached his mouth. The sigh of pure pleasure coming from Madison sent a sensation through him he hadn't expected. It was as if it were a memory, but he was sure he'd never met Madison before. Or had he? He studied her for a moment, looking at the curve of her cheeks and the blond hair that framed her face. She was beautiful sure, but in a solid and comfortable way. Nothing flashy that would draw you in, but intriguing in her own unique way. A face that looked much like a lot of women, but something about her seemed to indicate she'd be a woman who would be good to introduce to your parents. Of course, he'd never told his dad about any of the women in his life. Their relationship had been strained after his mother's death. His mom would have wanted to know about them, but she'd been gone for almost eight years. He pushed those memories of that dark time out of his mind.

He brought the pizza to his mouth and knew why she'd moaned like that. It took a lot of self-control to keep one of his own from slipping out. He took a second bite, as big as he could manage without shoving the whole thing in his mouth, and closed his eyes to focus on the flavors. As he chewed, a chuckle came from Madison, and he opened his eyes to see her grinning at him.

"Good, isn't it?"

Stephen shook his head. "Good doesn't even begin to describe it."

Madison nodded and took another bite then looked down at his notes. She wiped her lip to get some of the sauce then licked her finger, which Stephen thought was incredibly sexy.

"Do you have a Rosetta Stone for this?"

Stephen chuckled. "It's not that bad. You just have to think like me."

Madison rolled her eyes. "Whatever. We've got two-and-a-half hours to get this proposal top notch. How about you start sharing your scribbles, and we'll get this done." She put the pizza box on the corner of her desk then sat down. "Bring your chair over to this side where we can both see the screen."

Stephen didn't waste time grabbing his chair and setting it next to hers. She scooted over a little as he sat down, making him back up a bit to make sure he didn't come on too strong, and she seemed to relax. As the evening progressed, he was impressed with how quickly she took his ramblings and made a polished presentation. They finished at six forty-two with only a short pause for a run to the breakroom's fridge for Madison's private stash of Dr. Pepper.

Most women he dated would never have admitted they drank two cans of soda and ate that much pizza in a couple hours, and he was pleased Madison was comfortable enough with him to be herself. He couldn't wait to get to know more about her.

She looked at her clock and saved the presentation then sent a file of it to his email and one to Mr. Carlson. "I'll see you tomorrow."

Stephen reluctantly walked out the door and nodded to the night crew who were cleaning the office. He glanced around the area, still not sure where his office would be, and made a mental note to ask in the morning. Tonight, he'd go home and figure out a way to get Madison away from whomever she was meeting at seven.

Chapter Three

Mr. Carlson was smiling when Madison entered his office. He looked down at his monitor on the desk and nodded with approval. "I knew it was a good idea to put you two together. We'll be meeting with Doewins' reps this afternoon. Let Stephen know, will ya?"

Madison looked around the room, surprised she was being dismissed without them even going over the proposal in detail like they usually did. Was it because he thought, with Stephen as her project companion, he didn't have to double-check her work?

"I don't know where Mr. Kohalohini is at the moment. I'm not even sure where his office is."

Mr. Carlson lifted his head from his work and narrowed his brow at her. "Office, right." He pressed the button on his phone. "Mrs. Donahue."

His secretary's voice answered, "Yes, Mr.

Carlson?"

"Did you get the northwest corner conference room set up as an office for Mr. Kohali-ee, uh... Stephen?"

"Yes, there are a few things still on order but should arrive within the week." She paused for a moment. "Mr. Kohalohini is walking toward me. Would you like me to show him where the office will be?"

Mr. Carlson shook his head and spoke into the phone. "No need. I'll have Madison do it."

"Very good, sir," Kathryn's voice spoke. "Would you still like to see him this morning?"

"Sure, send him in." Mr. Carlson turned off his phone and turned his attention to the door.

Madison turned as well with mixed emotions. He was temporary but was being given a huge office while he was here, making the little green monster inside her roar with jealousy. When he opened the door and slipped inside, her heart hurt a little. After how well they'd worked together last night, she figured she could handle being in the same office with him, but seeing him again after going home to Milo reminded her of everything he'd just thrown away.

It would have been incredibly awkward for them to try working together if he had to explain why he'd dumped her so abruptly after they'd had sex. He had completely avoided her soon after, and it hurt. When she found out she was pregnant and told her parents about it, they'd been hugely disappointed in her and livid that Stephen was the father.

They'd always thought his carefree attitude and teenage antics were a bad influence on her. The fact that he was twenty to her eighteen made them even angrier, and they'd threatened to have him thrown in jail if she didn't stay away from him. Little did they know she had loved him from afar every summer he'd come, and that the last summer she'd finally had the courage to tell him how she felt. And she definitely didn't want to let him know how naive she had been, thinking he'd be the one she'd spend the rest of her life with. He obviously had just taken her willingness as a perk for that last summer in Montana, and then, once he'd gotten it, he'd been no longer interested. She should have known better.

As her pregnancy progressed, she'd wanted to contact him a couple months later to tell him about Milo, but her parents had made it clear what a bad choice he would be for a father. When he hadn't called or answered her calls — when she could sneak one in against her parents' wishes — she'd finally realized they were right. They'd shown her all the things they'd dug up on him by hiring a private investigator. Some of which he'd already told her himself, but she'd come to realize she didn't want him to help her raise a baby if he couldn't be responsible back then. But she just hadn't been able to give Milo up and had decided to raise him on her own, even though her parents had suggested placing the baby for adoption.

Her parents had agreed to help her with expenses and college tuition if she broke off all contact with Stephen, and now, seeing him here, she wondered if she'd made the right choice. He seemed to have grown up to be a responsible adult. Enough Mr. Carlson was hiring him to do what she could have done anyway, if he'd only given her the chance.

"I was just telling Madison what a fine job the two of you did on this proposal," Mr. Carlson said, smiling at Madison again. "You'll be meeting in the large conference room with Doewin at three. Madison will show you your office, and the two of you can fine tune this."

"Thank you, Mr. Carlson," Stephen said. "It was easy working with such talent." He smiled at Madison, and she was glad he hadn't winked. Most guys would have. The old Stephen would have.

"I'll see you both at two-thirty," Mr. Carlson said, turning away from them back to his files.

Madison knew when she'd been dismissed and turned around, not even bothering to wait for Stephen. If he didn't follow her, he ought to be smart enough to find a corner of the building. There were only three others besides the one Mr. Carlson was in, and the other two had conference rooms and distinct labels on the door.

Stephen caught up to her before she had passed Kathryn's desk, but he must have seen something of the secretary's that caught his attention. "Have you been to Hawaii, Mrs. Donahue?"

Kathryn's face lit up. "Yes, we just got back from a two-week vacation on the Big Island." She put the souvenir away. "I just can't stop thinking of it."

Stephen put his hand on his heart. "Everyone loves Hawaii. Did you island hop at all? I'm from Oahu."

As much as she wanted to leave him there, Madison wanted to hear more about Hawaii and what Kathryn had done. Besides, she had to go over the proposal with him once more to make sure they hadn't missed anything in their rush to get it ready.

Kathryn gushed over all the beautiful things they'd seen, and Stephen told her of his childhood, growing up in a small town just outside Honolulu.

Kathryn sighed. "Southern California is similar in many ways, but nothing can compare to the variety on Hawaii." She looked at Madison. "You really should go, dear."

"Someday," she agreed.

"I'd be happy to show you around," Stephen said.

Madison had heard that from him before and was sure this time was just as empty of a promise. She would never explore any of the Hawaiian Islands with him.

"No, thank you. I'll manage on my own." She took a step away from Kathryn's desk, refusing to look at either of them since she didn't want to feel guilty for the rudeness of her comment. "If you'll come with me, I'll show you where your office is."

She didn't wait for him, but he said his goodbyes to Kathryn, making her giggle with his "Aloha" as he walked away then easily matched Madison's stride on the way to his office. As soon as she opened the door, he whistled low. "Nice."

Madison kept her teeth tight together to prevent any more negativity from escaping her. Mr. Carlson had obviously prepared for Stephen's arrival, even if he hadn't told anyone else about it before yesterday. The desk was equipped with everything he needed from pencils, pens, computer, phone, and the project-display screens for wowing any clients who came to his office.

"Do you have any questions about your office, any of the equipment, or anything else about the agency?" Madison asked.

Stephen walked around the room and moved over to the large windows that gave him a perfect view of the city below. "Only one." He took a deep breath. "How do you like this view?"

Madison stared at his back then turned on her heel and marched out of the room without saying a word. Her mother's advice to never say anything mean warred with her desire to tell him exactly what she thought, and she knew if she stayed there a moment longer, she'd let him have it.

Stephen turned around to discover he was alone. Madison hadn't even said goodbye. He shrugged and wandered around the room for a minute, testing the height of the chair, moving a few things around on the desk for easier access, and turning on the computer to familiarize himself with it.

He found the file Madison had sent and looked it over. She had a knack for design, and that would help them as they pitched this afternoon.

After making sure he had what he would need and jotting down a note of what to get from the supply room, he grabbed his laptop and headed to her office. Since the door was open, he knocked on the doorframe then walked in. Madison's eyes narrowed at him, and he made a mental note to wait next time until she gave permission to enter.

She was a woman with rules, and if he wanted to get to know her, he needed to learn them and follow them.

"Are you available to go over the proposal?" Stephen asked.

Madison looked back at her computer. "I have a couple other things to take care of first. How about we meet in an hour? That should give us plenty of time."

Stephen nodded. "Sounds good." He grabbed one of the mini chocolates in the glass bowl on her desk, noting she'd refilled it from last night. When he moved the Snickers, he saw a Butterfinger. He snagged that one too, and when she didn't comment or respond in any way, he put that little bit of info in his mind. *Knock and wait for permission, but candy is okay.*

"Shall I come back here, or would you prefer to come to my office?" he asked as he reached the door.

Madison kept her eyes on her computer. "Here would be fine."

Stephen put another clue to her in his mind. *She prefers the familiar.*

Chapter Four

he nerve of that man. Madison fumed that he had taken her candy. Two of them, and he hadn't even asked. Her clients were polite enough to ask first, even though they were there for eating. It was just common courtesy. She forced thoughts of Stephen out of her head again.

If she didn't get this done soon, he'd be back again, thinking his project was the only thing worth working on. And if Mr. Carlson expected her to take over for Robert while he was gone, why was she still running the accounts? Doing all that extra work had been just to help out Robert, but she figured it was only for this project. She needed to catch up on all her clients' accounts and make sure everything was on schedule for the shoots and ad launches.

She immersed herself in the cereal company account and got everything lined up for the next few weeks. A knock on the door forced her to pull her eyes away from the computer screen. She shifted her gaze to see Stephen through the glass door. Why didn't he just come in? They had an appointment. She glanced at her clock to make sure it was time and waved him in.

As he opened the door, she finished a few minor things then opened the folder with their pitch for Doewin. She was torn between just handing it over to him or maintaining control of the pitch since she'd worked so hard on it. She didn't want to just give it away. Especially to him. She wanted to show Mr. Carlson she'd brought in this contract.

Adjusting her business smile on her face, she turned to him.

"So, who will head this discussion?" Stephen asked before she could speak.

Madison's eyes widened. Was he really asking her opinion, or just trying to stake his claim. Oh, she wished she knew him better. Or not at all. The past was eating at her, and she hated the way it made her feel lost.

"You're supposed to be the expert. What do you suggest?"

"I say we do this together. You present your ideas since they'll be expecting you, and I can build on it and wrap up the presentation. Fill in anything you might miss. It will also give me a chance to watch how your company works with potential clients. That way I'll know if we need to work on anything like that."

Madison nodded. "Sounds reasonable."

They discussed the presentation for a while, then Stephen leaned forward and grabbed another one of her Butterfingers. What was with the man? Why couldn't he pick one of the other kinds? She would have to stop filling the candy jar to keep his thieving fingers out of it, but that thought made her annoyed, and she fumed inside.

"What do you say, Madison?"

She lifted her head and stared into his eyes, completely lost on where the conversation had gone. "I'm sorry, what?"

"I wanted to know if you'd like to do lunch. I'm starving." He grabbed another candy bar, but at least this time it was a Snickers. "I always work better on a full stomach."

Madison shook her head. "No thank you. I brought something from home because I planned on working through lunch again. I've got a lot of accounts that have been neglected with this Doewin thing."

"Maybe another time," Stephen said.

Madison didn't respond but stood and motioned for Stephen to leave the office ahead of her. "I'll see you in the conference room."

Once he was out the door, she walked to the

breakroom hoping he would head to his office or go out to one of the nearby restaurants for lunch like he'd indicated, but he followed her.

"I think I'll check the vending machine," he said when she looked at him for an explanation of why he was behind her.

She nodded, grabbed her leftovers from the fridge, heated them in the microwave for less than a minute, and left the breakroom as fast as she could before he tried talking to her again.

Stephen couldn't decide if anything in the vending machine was worth buying. The sandwiches didn't look very fresh, and he wasn't in the mood for any of the frozen entrees. He wished Madison would have agreed to go to lunch with him. Or that he had gone alone. Instead, he'd had the stupid idea to follow her into the breakroom in an attempt to spend more time with her. He turned around to see where she'd sat and was surprised to find himself alone.

He hadn't even heard her leave. This woman was good at disappearing.

He was going to have to step up his game and figure out a way to talk to her. Something about her was so familiar, and he wished he could place it. Maybe it was just that she was the kind of person he'd always wanted in his life. Beautiful and kind. And the fact that she wasn't threatened by having him observe the project she'd been working on. Showed she was confident, and that was what an ad exec needed. Yet she'd seemed relieved he was there to take over and let her get back to what she preferred doing. He'd have to stretch her. Mold her into the best Carlson had. She did have talent, though. He wouldn't have to work too hard to get her to the point she could take the business in the right direction.

It was refreshing to work with someone of her transparency and openness.

He hoped they'd be able to collaborate on many of the new accounts he'd be working on. Not that Robert didn't seem capable, but Madison was younger, and she'd be able to adjust to the changing market easier.

He punched in the number for one of the less-offensive-looking sandwiches and sighed when he opened the package. Yeah, roast beef on white bread with a pathetic slice of tomato and some sort of white cheese really wasn't going to cut it. He glanced at his watch and called for some spicy Indian curry.

He arrived to the conference room at 2:15 so he could be early and get set up, but Madison was already there with the presentation out and the flat screen opened to the slide show.

This woman was on fire.

Chapter Five

As the representatives from Doewin arrived, Madison greeted them and introduced them to Stephen. He schmoozed them right out the door, and Madison wondered if he was going to keep things the way they'd planned. After the initial introductions were over, and Stephen showed them to their seats, Madison turned on the screen and began the presentation.

Stephen didn't take over exactly, but he added comments with each slide, going into more detail than what they had gone over just hours ago. As the presentation continued, Stephen got more and more animated, taking her ideas and elaborating on them. As he got into it, Madison could see that his enthusiasm was contagious, and the representatives from Doewin were practically eating out of his hands. The woman especially.

They'd be signing with Carlson Agency for sure, but Madison fumed inside. How could he do this to her? Mr. Carlson looked impressed with Stephen, yet rarely even glanced at Madison, making her fear she might be in jeopardy of losing footing with her boss, yet the ideas had almost all been hers in the first place.

As the presentation wrapped up, Madison felt like her only role in the whole thing had morphed into changing screens while Stephen got the clients laughing at the potential commercials they could do. She admired and hated him for it.

Mr. Carlson leaned forward in his seat and took control of the conversation as Madison closed the presentation. "As you can see, you'd be in good hands with Carlson Ad Agency. What do you say?"

The woman glanced at the man to the side of her. He nodded, and she leaned back and crossed her long legs under the table. "I'm very impressed and believe we can go far together."

"Wonderful news, Ms. Daws," Mr. Carlson said. "We've got a standard contract written. Madison will get it to you. Have your legal department check it over, and we'll meet again tomorrow to sign if you're in agreement."

Ms. Daws' eyes widened in surprise. Most clients expressed appreciation that they weren't bullied into signing anything right away and always came back to say the contract was fair and generous. It was something that made Madison happy to work for Carlson Ad Agency.

Stephen looked surprised as well. Before he could speak and ruin their tradition, Madison stood and shook hands with Mr. Gregor and began walking toward the door. "If you have any questions, give me a call. We're looking forward to working together." As Madison pulled out her wallet for the business card, her driver's license slipped out and fell to the floor.

"Thank you, Madison." The representatives from Doewin took the business card, shook her hand, and then left the room.

Stephen, out of nowhere, bent down to pick up the driver's license and Madison cringed. As his fingers reached it, he slowed down and took a moment to lift it. His gaze never left the card, and Madison had a horrible feeling he was checking out her weight.

She'd lied on it of course, but it still wasn't something she wanted him to think about, or even notice. Madison held her hand out for the license, and Stephen's eyes met hers, searching her face in a way that made her uncomfortable.

"Bea?" His voice was soft and unsure, nothing like it had been moments before during the presentation.

Madison closed her eyes. Of course he would have seen her legal name. And now he'd finally made the connection as to who she was. Did she admit she remembered him, or pretend she was just now coming to put two and two together?

"Yes," Madison said. "My name is Beatrice. I go by Madison at work, though."

"You're the Bea from King, Montana, where my grandparents lived."

Madison scrambled once more, trying to decide the best way to deal with this mess. It would have been much better for him to have never remembered her. Now they'd have all that awkward stuff from their past.

"Yes." Madison sighed. "One and the same."

Stephen's gaze roamed her face and hair. "You were brunette back then. And a skinny little—" He stopped short and blushed and cleared his throat. She'd been a little on the awkward side and a bit of a late bloomer. "You remember me, right?"

Madison struggled to keep her emotions in check. Oh, how she wished she could forget it all. She nodded slowly. "I remember."

"Oh my goodness. I can't believe I didn't recognize you after all the fun we…" He cleared his throat. "I feel so foolish. But I'm so excited to see you again. I can't believe we're actually working together. We really need to catch up."

Before Madison could find a way to avoid the requested date she knew he was going to ask for, Mr.

Carlson interrupted. "You two know each other?"

Stephen cleared his throat. "We dated a few years back for a while. Knew each other as teens."

Madison looked at Mr. Carlson, who raised a brow then looked them both over. "You both good to work together?"

Madison nodded. "Yes. There will be no problems at work."

"Good. I'd hate to think the past might interfere with your future here. You two are a perfect team." He patted Madison on the shoulder then did the same to Stephen as he positioned himself between the two.

How could he have thought that? The whole presentation had ended up with Stephen taking control of it all, talking over her in every one of her ideas, and she'd succumbed to it without doing anything to show she still knew what she was doing. Mr. Carlson had never seemed like a sexist kind of guy who didn't value a woman's input.

"I have a wonderful idea," Mr. Carlson continued. "I'd like you two to join efforts while Stephen's here. I think with you both coming up with ideas and presenting them like this, we can bring in more big-name companies. Madison, I know you can keep up with the accounts for a while, but I'll look into hiring someone to assist in that aspect. In fact, Robert might be able to do a lot of that kind of stuff from home.

You can take it back when he returns. I'll run it by him, but I want the two of you to brainstorm on the potential client list I showed you. You've got great chemistry together, and I'd love to see how fast our business can explode with you two."

Madison closed her eyes. Explode was right. There was no way she could work with Stephen like that. Too messy, and how could she keep Milo a secret if she was always with him? She didn't want to explore those feeling for him, knowing he wouldn't return them, or if he ever did, she didn't trust them to stay. He'd tossed her away so easily before, how could she survive the hurt if it happened again? Besides, his time here was temporary. Just like it had been in King.

Chapter Six

$\mathcal{S}$ tephen stared at the computer screen in his office. He couldn't believe Madison was Bea from years ago. He'd thought of her on occasion, but had usually ended up remembering the last time his family had been complete. They'd found out his mother had cancer right after returning to Hawaii after finalizing the sale of his grandparents' farm. Her cancer had already advanced to stage four, and there had been nothing they could do. It had been quick and brutal, stealing his mother's life away from his family.

And though he'd wanted to contact Bea, her parents had made it clear she was off limits. They'd caught him sneaking out of her house one night and had threatened to charge him with everything they could think of if he didn't clear out and stay away from her. They'd listed all his faults, knowing from his grandparents about some of the trouble he'd gotten into at home and why he'd been sent to King, Montana, every summer. They were still livid about Bea and him getting arrested for throwing water balloons at a car during the Fourth of July parade the summer before. How were they supposed to know the cold water would shatter the hot windshield?

He'd tried calling and sneaking over to see her, but her parents had taken her on a shopping trip in preparation for college, but he knew it had been to get her away from him until he'd gone back home.

He'd lost his phone in the ocean when he'd gone out boating to come to terms with his mother's diagnosis and hadn't had Bea's cell phone number anywhere else. Her parents wouldn't answer the house phone when he'd tried calling either. But Bea had never tried calling or finding him, making him think their time together had meant nothing to her.

He should have never let her parents run him off, and if he hadn't gotten distracted with his mother's illness, he would have contacted her sooner. By the time he'd been ready to track her down, he'd figured she would have already been off to college dating someone. He'd looked for her on all the social media sites, but Bea Perry didn't exist. And no wonder, if she'd changed her name to Madison.

She must have thought he was a complete jerk, or just a horny guy after a summer fling. But now that he'd run into Bea again and was working with her for a few months, he was going to have to make things right.

He thought back over the last twenty-four hours and understood a little bit of her hesitance. She'd remembered him. That had to be a good thing, right? He'd meant enough to her that she hadn't just dismissed him completely when they'd lost touch.

And seeing the type of woman she was today, blended with the memories surfacing from that summer, he really wanted to see where things could go.

But how could he go about it? He was sure he was in the hole after having not recognized her at first. That would be hard to come back from. And by working together, he'd have to go slow so she didn't get skittish or think he was harassing her. He'd have to check the company policy with HR to make sure it was okay to date.

He hoped so. He very much wanted to rekindle what they once had.

Madison flipped through the potential client list, not even registering the names. Her mind was on Stephen and the look of complete surprise when he realized who she was. She wasn't sure if he had been impressed or horrified. This would make for a very uncomfortable couple of months.

He was good here. She admitted that. And with his talents and her familiarity with the company, they could really do some good things for Carlson Ad Agency. Besides, she was a professional. She could keep things on the business level. It was never a good idea to date a colleague. And she really didn't want to bring Milo in to the mix. Staying away from Stephen was the best thing she could do.

As she thought of him again, she sighed. If she were truthful, she kind of did want to see where things would lead. But she'd worked too hard in the company to let something temporary like Stephen get in the way.

She really didn't know the man. So much could have changed over the last eight years. Though, when they'd been together that summer, he had seemed kind and reliable, nothing like her parents had accused him of being. Yet the moment he left, she'd obviously no longer been important to him.

Madison focused her attention on the potential clients only to be distracted again when Stephen knocked on her door. He held his laptop up. "Do you have time to go over the list?"

"That's what I'm doing now. Have a seat."

Stephen entered the room, grabbed the chair he'd

used yesterday, and brought it around to her side where he'd sat as they'd worked. He didn't bring it too close, for which Madison was thankful, but it was still disconcerting to have him near.

Instead of opening his laptop, he set it on her desk and looked at the open file on hers. "I've heard of a few of these companies. Some I've had contact with, and it should be easy enough to bring them to Carlson."

"That's good," Madison said. "I know Robert made some initial inquiries to these companies, and a lot of them showed some interest in hearing what we could do. I'll follow up with them." She sighed at the workload ahead of her. She still had to take care of the client accounts since Robert wasn't ready to take on that part yet. Hopefully, she'd still be able to leave the office on time each night. Though, Karen would be good about keeping Milo later, if it came to that.

It would be easy enough to train Carrie to replace her if Robert couldn't do it. Carrie had been doing a lot to assist her while she'd helped Robert. Madison would have to suggest her to Mr. Carlson.

"I think I've got time to contact a few of these companies before the end of the business day if I get started right now." Madison hoped he'd take the hint and leave so she didn't have to spend more time with him at that moment.

Stephen pushed his chair back away from her desk but didn't stand. "I'll work on some suggestions for pitches."

Madison nodded and turned to her work, but the man still didn't take the hint and leave. Instead, he did what she was dreading and brought up the past.

"Don't you think we should talk about things?"

She could divert the topic and claim they had already discussed how they would be working together, but he was right. They needed to air out the past and make rules for how things would go in the future. And she might as well start it out on the right track and set the rules.

"You're right. We'll be working closely together now. We're both adults and are capable of keeping what happened between us in the past. It's over and done. No hard feelings at all, and if we keep this strictly business, everything will be fine."

Stephen nodded slowly. "Right. We're both professionals. It was so long ago, and we were so young." He stopped talking and reached for his laptop. "We'll need to carve out a few hours each day where we can plan and brainstorm. Then, as the clients start coming in for your pitches, we'll arrange schedules." He stood and took hold of the back of the chair as he walked around the desk. "What time of day would work better for you? I know the mornings will be the best time to reach out to the companies, but by mid-morning and early afternoon, I'll be flexible."

"I'm usually swamped all day, but I think I can make the afternoons more open as well. Should we plan for three o'clock these next few days and see how it goes?"

Stephen nodded as he returned her chair to its usual location. "Perfect," he said. "See you tomorrow." He gave her a smile before leaving. As his back disappeared around the doorframe, Madison couldn't help feeling disappointed that he was gone, even though she'd hoped he'd leave almost from the moment he'd arrived.

She was never going to make this work, and if it was that easy for him to dismiss what they'd had, she didn't want to be forced to work with him more than she had to. Maybe someone else at the agency would be a better fit for this position so she could stay with what she knew and was good at.

Chapter Seven

$\mathcal{S}$tephen didn't know what to think. He'd been
shot down before he'd even made a move,
and it hurt. He wasn't used to being completely
ignored, and as memories of his time with Bea — or
Madison as she now liked to be called — returned, he
wanted to renew that relationship.

But work had to come first. If he could convince
her they were a good team, he would have time to start
wearing down her defenses. He had time, and it would
be good for him to practice patience.

He thought back to that summer after he'd turned
twenty, trying to remember things about Bea that
would help him win her over now. They'd spent lots of
time watching movies in her parents' basement. Her
family's land was only a mile from his grandparents'
farm, and they'd been friends every summer.

He should have tried to find her sooner, but by

the time he'd come out of his depression at losing his mom, he'd already been two terms into his sophomore year at college and was trying to just keep his head above water in his classes to keep his scholarship.

He leaned back against the chair and closed his eyes, visualizing how much she'd changed. Her body was perfectly proportioned and didn't look overly thin like so many women thought was ideal. No, in his opinion, the curves and soft flesh was better, and he appreciated how she looked. He'd have to be careful to not reach for her like he'd been allowed to that summer.

Their relationship had been interesting, being friends during the summer months when he came to help on the farm. After his grandparents had both passed away within months of each other, leaving the farm to his mother who couldn't run it, they'd come that last summer to prepare it to sell. His mom had tried to convince him to take the farm, but it had never interested him enough to stay. Bea had been the only reason he could tolerate the small ranch town, and she hadn't planned to stay there.

He'd always enjoyed Bea's company, knowing she never judged him for his mistakes, but just accepted him for who he was. She'd made him feel valuable and worthwhile. That summer after she'd graduated, she'd allowed things to get more serious, and he was thrilled to know she felt that way about him.

They'd never been romantic during any of the previous summers, just enjoying each other's company in the lonely ranch town, but something about that last year had appeared to be powerful for both of them. And with her finally out of high school, it seemed acceptable to develop a stronger relationship, even if it was just for the summer. He'd known it would be the last time he would return, and she'd been planning on leaving for college as well, with the intent to never come back. Apparently, she'd made good on it. She'd been working at Carlson's four years, hired before she could have even finished college. She'd no doubt worked hard to get where she was and seeing her so valuable here made him feel proud.

They had a lot to catch up on, but it would be tricky, and he would need to look at this like any other business endeavor.

Madison closed her laptop and tidied her desk in preparation to leave for the night. She couldn't wait to get home and relax. She wanted a long bubble bath but knew that would have to wait until Milo was in bed. She glanced at the clock, knowing she'd make it in time to pick him up before her sister had to take off. Karen was a godsend, and Madison knew she was the only reason she'd survived these last eight years as a single parent.

Madison locked her office and adjusted the strap of her purse over her shoulder in time to see Stephen step out of his office. She ducked her head, not wanting to make eye contact with him, and headed down the hall at a quick pace, hoping to avoid seeing him on the way out.

The elevator took forever, and Madison cringed when she felt him come up to the side of her. "Mind if I ride down with you?"

Who asked if they could ride the same elevator? And was she supposed to give him an answer? Madison shrugged as if it didn't matter and wished she'd chosen the stairs. She'd have to do that next time. As the elevator opened, Stephen waited for her to step in first, then as he joined her, she realized once again how large the man was. She couldn't reach the button to push her floor for the parking garage without touching him, so she stayed back to wait and see which one he picked.

He pressed the same level as hers, and she almost wished it had been a different one so she wouldn't have to walk any further with him than necessary. All the memories warred against her anger and sense of betrayal.

Stephen turned to her. "How's your family?"

Madison blinked in surprise. "They're good."

"Do you see them often?"

"My sister lives close. I see her pretty regularly." Madison pressed her lips together. She saw her every weekday. She should have asked how his family was but didn't want to encourage him to keep talking.

"Do you ever go back home to King?" Stephen asked.

"Not much. My parents have sold the cows and just raise hay now. They come visit us kids more often now that their time is freer."

"Do you miss King?" Stephen asked just as the elevator reached their floor.

Madison met his eyes. "Not really. I don't think fondly on much of anything there anymore." She stepped through the door and pressed the unlock button on her car to get inside and away from him as quickly as possible. He didn't follow her, and she was glad, but as she got in, guilt washed over her at her words. She shouldn't have snapped at him like that, but she really wasn't in the mood to reminisce about their past.

When she got to her sister's, she grinned to see Milo watching out the window for her. The little man was so precious to her and she could at least be grateful Stephen had given her something so wonderful out of something so heartbreaking. A tiny voice in the back of her mind told her she should tell him, but a stronger voice rebelled at the idea. Stephen had made his choice and disappeared from her life; she didn't owe him anything, least of all parental rights to a child he didn't even know existed.

Karen opened the door and smiled at Madison as she walked up the front walk and prepped herself to meet the enthusiastic hug from her son. Milo was too heavy for her to lift often, and the thought of him no longer being a baby but a little boy tugged at her heart.

And because he looked more and more like his father, having the man back in her life this way was making it hard to keep her emotions in check. Madison wiped a tear from her eye. She took his hand in hers to go back inside and gather his things and help clean up his toys before they left.

Karen patted Milo on the back. "Go on in and grab your stuff. I need to talk to your mom for a second."

Milo looked between his aunt and mom with wide eyes. "I didn't do anything bad." He met his mom's eyes with pleading in his. "I wasn't naughty, I promise."

Karen giggled. "Of course not, buddy. You've been a perfect gentleman. This isn't about you. It's a mommy thing."

Milo nodded happily and ducked past Karen's arms and rushed inside, hollering to his cousins that he had a few more minutes to play. Madison chuckled and shook her head. "What did he do?"

Karen glanced back. "He didn't do anything. He's been perfect." She met Madison's eyes. "It's what he said. Told me his mommy cried all night last night. And I see you wiping tears now. Something's going on."

Madison's eyes misted again, and she leaned into her sister, longing for someone to take care of her for a moment. Karen wrapped her in a hug. "What's wrong, sweetie?"

"I saw Stephen again."

Karen pulled back a little. "Stephen? Milo's dad?" she whispered.

Madison nodded. "He's been hired as a consultant at Carlson."

"You're kidding. What did you do?" Karen pulled her into the house and guided her over to the couch.

"I showed him where is office is, gave him the tour of the place, and had to work with him on a pitch." Madison put her hands over her face. "And now Mr. Carlson wants us to work together all the time. He's supposed to train me on how to bring more business to the company, but everything he's suggested so far is exactly what I would do anyway if Mr. Carlson would just let me." She yanked her hands down and turned to

Karen. "I can't work with him. I told Stephen I didn't want to talk about anything that happened in the past."

"What did he say about Milo?" Karen asked.

Madison peeked toward the room Milo had gone to play. "I didn't tell him." She looked at her sister, hoping to find support and not condemnation. "He never answered any of my calls, emails, or letters. Nothing I did to contact him worked. I don't know if he even knows, and I want to keep it that way."

"But he's Milo's father. Don't you think he deserves to know?"

Madison shook her head. "No. He didn't care enough about me. Why should I let him have anything to do with Milo?"

Karen reached out gently to take Madison's hand in hers. "Sweetie, I think he has a right to know. And if he is a nice guy and is good at what he does, don't you think it would be good for Milo to know his daddy?"

Madison pulled her hand back and crossed her arms around herself. "He isn't his daddy. He might be the biological father, but he's missed out on too much to be a daddy. Besides, Milo has Jason to look up to."

Karen nodded slowly. "And Jason loves him more than anything, but an uncle isn't the same thing."

Madison glared at Karen. "Whose side are you on?"

"I'm not picking sides, sweetie, but if I had to, it would be Milo's. I think you ought to at least consider telling Stephen about him, find out if he'd like to have a chance to get to know the son he has. It's not like you have to marry him or even date him. You can keep it professional and still be merciful to the man."

Madison's eyes burned with unshed tears. She'd done this all alone for so long she didn't want to give him a chance. He'd blown it years ago, and even now, it was obvious he hadn't had feelings for her.

Karen's voice broke through her thoughts. "At least think about it. You don't have to make the decision tonight but don't shoot down the idea completely. Look at your rights, and his."

Madison's eyes widened. "Do you think he'd try to take him away from me?"

"No, and I don't think a court would allow that anyway, but if you don't make the choice to involve him, and he finds out on his own, he would have a stronger case against you than if you let him know."

Madison nodded, wishing she'd never met the man, but a moment later when Milo came in with his little backpack full of books, announcing he'd cleaned up in the toy room, her heart softened, and she was fiercely glad she had her little guy. She would give it some thought, knowing Milo was such a sweet boy, and Stephen deserved to at least know of him.

Chapter Eight

As the days progressed, Stephen knew he was going to really enjoy working there, but it was going to be hard to break through Madison's tough shell. Every time they met together to go over client proposals and pitch to the potential clients, she was all business, with no chance for him to just chat with her. And as soon as they were done, she left the office in a rush and rebuffed his attempts at bringing up their summers together.

In fact, every time he mentioned them, she stiffened and changed the subject. He would try again today and thought he finally had something that would work.

He'd brought some macadamia nuts. She'd loved them when his family had brought them with from Hawaii to his grandparents. He'd started packing a bottle for her during his teens since they spent so much time together after the chores were done, and she'd eaten a bunch the first day, then rationed them to last for most of the summer. One year he'd brought a second bottle and given it to her as a gift halfway through July, and she'd kissed him for the first time that night.

As he knocked on her office door and waited for her to wave him in, he moved the bottle from one hand to the other, watching her through the glass side window. She sighed and waved him in, and he opened the door. Her eyes fell on the nuts, and she raised an eyebrow. He placed them on her desk.

"For you."

"Why?" Madison asked.

"I just thought you might like some. If I remember right, they were some of your favorites."

Madison's eyes softened, and she smiled. "I haven't had them for years."

"Why?" Stephen asked.

Her face took on a look of panic that was quickly replaced by sadness for a moment. "It's not important. Thanks."

"No problem." He knew better than to open them and get one out, so he helped himself to another one of her mini candy bars on the desk.

She watched him for a moment, her eyes hiding something, and he wondered if maybe he shouldn't just take the candies. He contented himself with only one and opened his laptop to get ready for the client list, but Madison hadn't stopped looking at the macadamias.

She took a slow breath then pushed them back. "I do appreciate the offer, but I can't take these."

Stephen frowned. "Why not?" The hurt in her eyes angered him, and he crossed his arms over his chest. "Get over it, Madison. I'm sorry about what happened. I'm sorry you're angry at me for whatever reason, but we had good times before. I can't believe you're being so petty as to reject every attempt at me being friendly. I don't expect you to jump into my bed. In fact, I don't think we were ready for that even when it did happen. Grow up and just take the stupid nuts."

Madison's eyes went from sadness to shock to anger. She pushed the nuts back to him, stood up, and leaned across her desk.

"I can't accept these nuts because my son has a severe tree nut allergy, and if I ate them, I wouldn't be able to kiss him goodnight."

Stephen's jaw dropped open, and he scrambled for something to say in response.

"So I'm sorry if that ruins your attempt to get me back into your bed, but I don't think I ever want to go down that road again."

She towered over him as he sat in his chair. Part

of him wanted to stand up and confront her, but the only thing that he could think of was the startling news she was a mother.

"I'm sorry, Madison. I didn't realize you were married or had a kid. I never would have..." He trailed off as her eyes turned dark.

"Not everyone who has a kid is married. Sometimes the father isn't interested in those responsibilities." She turned away from him, covering her mouth as angry tears threatened to spill from her eyes.

"No, you're right. Not every mother is married. And I'm sorry that the guy was such a scum."

Madison burst into a strange laughter and turned back to him, her mouth covered, but she shook her head in disbelief as she stared at him.

Understanding hit him hard, and he was glad he was sitting. "I'm the father?"

"If you ever would have called me after you left, you'd know that." She pushed away from her desk and grabbed her purse. "But you wanted nothing to do with me then, and I want nothing to do with you now." She marched around the other side of the desk, completely skirting around him. "You'll have to finish this pitch on your own. I can't be here right now."

She closed the door, leaving him in her office alone to pick up all the pieces.

Madison walked blindly through the hallway toward the elevator then changed her mind and veered to the left and took the stairs. She didn't want to risk being trapped in an elevator with him right now. She'd blown it and had blurted out all the hurt and anger she'd felt toward him and dumped the news of a child. Then left without giving him a chance to say anything.

Not that she wanted to listen to his excuses on why he wasn't available to her. Her mind had conjured up all kinds of things. He'd died in the plane going back to Hawaii, he'd been eaten by a shark, he'd fallen into a volcano — no matter that his island wasn't an active volcano anymore.

They'd only slept together a few times, but it was enough to get her pregnant. She hadn't wanted to stay in King, Montana as a single mom. When her sister Karen asked her to come live with them to help out with their newest baby, Madison had jumped at the chance. It was a good way for her to learn a bit about kids so she could decide if she wanted to keep the baby or give it up for adoption. She'd gone and had never tried tracking Stephen down again.

And now, she'd made a life for herself, had a

wonderful neighborhood to live in, a small home near her sister, and a job that could support both of them. She didn't need Stephen now. And Milo was doing just fine.

Her heels clicked on the steps as she continued her descent to the parking garage. She should have told Mr. Carlson she was leaving, but it was only two hours early, and she'd get the work done later. Right now, she couldn't think straight enough to be an effective employee.

Madison pushed open the door to the parking level and felt the warm air wash over her. It smelled of tires and new paint, but the exhaust fans helped keep the air breathable. She headed straight for her car and climbed in then headed for Jessie's Grill. She was long overdue for a monster calorie splurge.

By the time her order arrived, she was near tears again and tried to drown her pain in the pleasure of the food. It helped. Halfway through the burger, she felt her phone vibrate in her purse. She wiped the grease and sauce off her fingers and pulled out her phone.

The text was from a number she didn't recognize, but the first words made it obvious who it was.

Bea, we have to talk.

She pushed the off button, not willing to answer. At least not yet. Let him stew about this. And she didn't want to hear the constant vibration as he texted over and over again. She shoved a cheese fry coated in special sauce into her mouth and followed it closely with another few before moving over to the extra-large Dr. Pepper.

She knew she'd probably make herself sick, but that would be tons better than the guilt and remorse she'd begun to feel.

"How could I be so stupid?" she whispered to her food, ignoring the looks from the strangers around her. She shoved the rest of the food away from her but kept the drink, bringing it up to her forehead and pressing the cold paper cup against her brow.

She would now have to tell him more about Milo. Let him know about his son, and who knew what Stephen would do about it.

Would he want to have visitation rights? Would he demand his parental rights, or worse, would he want nothing to do with Milo? She had to protect her little boy at all costs.

If Stephen was willing to meet him, she had to make sure Milo understood how the relationship would go, but she wanted to know Stephen's intentions before she let them get within twenty feet of each other. And from the look of shock and horror on his face when he realized her child was his, she didn't hold much hope for good things.

She didn't expect them to become a family, but

after Karen's advice to think about how much it would mean for Milo to know his father, she had to admit it was a good idea. Milo hadn't asked too many questions over the years about where his dad was, but he was aware things were different for him and that he didn't have a daddy but had Uncle Jason.

Madison grabbed a napkin and wiped her nose then folded it carefully to get the tears around her eyes. She took a long slow drink of her soda then pulled her phone back out. When it powered back on, she had five missed calls and text after text, asking for her to talk to him.

He might be almost eight years too late, but at least he was making an attempt now.

Chapter Nine

Stephen paced his office, debating on whether to try calling again or not. She was obviously pissed at him and wasn't ready to talk, but he knew he had to keep trying. He had a son he knew nothing about, and he wasn't going to let that slip away from him.

She'd accused him of not trying to contact her, but every call he'd made to her parents' house always ended in a hang-up the second they'd known who it was, or the phone had just rung without even being picked up by their ancient answering machine. And had she really tried to call him? His new phone had the same number, so if she'd called his cell, he should have gotten those calls.

He rubbed his hands through his hair, feeling horrible, knowing he'd done nothing to help her. And she'd kept his child instead of aborting it or placing it for adoption. A son. He would be just over seven years old. Stephen didn't have much experience with children other than his cousins, since he didn't have any siblings. Though Hawaiian families were traditionally very large and close-knit, his was different.

His mother had met his dad while she'd been vacationing on Oahu. They'd fallen in love right away, and she hadn't gone back home to the ranch, but instead had eloped with his dad. When he'd asked why he didn't have brothers or sisters, his mom had told him he'd been a miracle baby.

He didn't have a family, and he wanted one. Yet the child he did have didn't even know him. Anger at the injustice of it all boiled low and steady. She had to talk to him. She couldn't keep this from him anymore.

There was still an hour before he could technically leave, but he was tempted to go search for her anyway. He had no clue where to go, and though he'd found her phone number on company records, he didn't think she'd look kindly on him showing up at her house. He was completely at her mercy, and the feeling unsettled him.

He pulled the chair out from his desk and sat down, trying to focus on the work in front of him, but it was difficult to keep his mind from Bea. They'd been so young, it was hard to imagine her being a mother the way he remembered her from that summer. She would have been a fabulous mother. She was kind and sweet and caring, but it never should have happened that soon.

He grabbed his phone and typed another text, but before he could hit send, her first response came through.

I need time. We can talk tomorrow at lunch.

Stephen's heart leapt with joy, then fear gripped him. What could he possibly say to her? He would let her take the lead and see what she was willing to do. He erased the text he'd been preparing and sent a simple reply.

Thank you.

Madison pulled into her sister's driveway and eased herself out of her car, wishing she'd stopped eating sooner. She hoped eating at Jessie's wouldn't be ruined for her because of associating it with this whole mess with Stephen. She looked up to the window, hoping to see Milo's bright eyes watching her, but she was early so he wouldn't be expecting her at the moment. She brought the take-out bag full of his favorite fries and felt like a horrible mother that it was all she planned on feeding him for dinner.

When she got to the door and Karen answered, her sister took one look at her and pulled her into a hug then led her to the couch. "Spill."

"I told him," Madison said with a sigh.

"And?"

"And then I left him in my office and went and binged at Jessie's."

"Uh oh. It went that bad, huh? What did he say?"

Madison shook her head. "I didn't give him a chance. I was so angry at something he'd said it all came out in an angry blast, and now I don't know what to do."

"You haven't talked to him since that?" Karen asked.

"No. He sent a bunch of texts and called a couple times, but I ignored it." She hung her head. "I finally sent one saying I needed a little time, and we could talk tomorrow, but what am I going to tell him? I don't want him to feel like he has to be a part of Milo's life if he doesn't want to be, but I don't want him to think he can't. You were right. Milo needs to know him, and he's not a creep, so I'm not worried about that. I'm just worried about him not caring."

Karen took a moment to answer. "You can take it as slow as you need to. Find out what he wants to do so you'll know where to go from there."

Madison nodded, and a squeal of joy came

through the doorway as Milo spotted her. "Momma!"

She opened her arms and caught him as he climbed onto the couch with her. She snuggled him close, relishing the joy he brought into her life. The unconditional love of a child should be experienced by everyone, and she was glad it had been hers.

She gathered Milo up and handed him the bag of fries. "You can eat these in the car on our way home, okay, buddy?"

Milo's face lit up, and he ran to get his bag and rushed out the door hollering as he left. "See you tomorrow, Aunt Karen."

"See ya, kiddo," Karen hollered back, a huge grin on her face. She looked at Madison. "He cracks me up. Good luck tomorrow. Let me know how it goes."

Madison nodded and walked out to join Milo, who was bouncing around by the car. "Can I really eat them before we get home? In the car?"

Madison giggled at his enthusiasm. "I think I can trust you to not make a mess. You are getting to be pretty big. I bet you could handle it really easy."

Milo stood a little straighter, throwing his shoulders back. "I am big. I'll be a big daddy like Uncle Jason someday."

Madison's smile fell just a little. He really did need a father figure. Now if only she knew what kind of relationship Stephen could provide for him, it would make tomorrow's meeting a lot less intimidating.

Chapter Ten

*S*tephen had seen Madison for only a moment this morning as she left Mr. Carlson's office, so he knew she was here, but lunch was still an hour away, and he was dying to talk to her. She hadn't glared at him as she passed but had given him a sad smile, making him feel like no matter what he did or said today, he wouldn't come out of this unscathed.

As he looked at the clock, he realized he didn't know where they were meeting for lunch. And would they eat, or just talk? He pulled out his phone and composed a text, hoping it wouldn't go unanswered.

Where would you like to meet for lunch?

The reply came back quicker than he expected.

We could go out, bring our client list, and make it a working lunch in addition to the other.

Good idea. How soon are you free to leave?

Her text took longer this time, and he looked at

his list of things to do, wondering how much he could put off until tomorrow and what he'd have to stay late to finish.

We could go now if that works.

Stephen stared at the phone, surprised she wasn't putting him off.

Meet me at the elevator?

Her follow-up text came moments later.

Give me five minutes.

It took him seven minutes to get to the elevator, but Madison met his eyes and smiled softly then pressed the elevator button. When they stepped inside the elevator, he asked, "Do you have a place picked out?"

Madison nodded. "I was thinking of a little sandwich shop a couple blocks down. It's got good food, and the booths are tucked away and quiet. Plus they won't mind if we stay awhile and discuss work after we're done."

"Sounds perfect," Stephen said. The elevator reached the lobby floor of the office building, and Stephen waited for Madison to exit first. He caught up to her side, and they walked in silence to the sandwich place. He let her order first to see how it was done then picked out his toppings. She'd already paid for her meal before the kid behind the glass sneeze-guard had finished making his. He sighed in disappointment but paid then joined her in a small booth in the far corner.

She set her sandwich on the table then reached into her purse and pulled out a small, framed photograph and passed it over slowly to him. Stephen reached for it, feeling more nervous than he thought he would. He'd be seeing his son for the first time, and he wished he had a moment to prepare himself.

The kid looking back at him could have been himself when he was little. The eyes were obviously his, but Stephen could see Madison's features in his face as well. His smile was wide and showed a gap between his front teeth from losing one. The cheeks still looked round, and his eyes sparkled as if the photographer had caught him in a laugh. Stephen's heart beat harder for a few minutes, and a nervous ball formed in the pit of his stomach.

How could he have missed out on this, and now that he knew of the boy, what was he supposed to do? He wanted to be a part of his life, but how?

Madison watched Stephen closely, hoping for a clue to his emotions as he studied the picture of their son. His eyes devoured the photo, but he didn't speak for the longest time. When he finally pulled his gaze away and looked at her, he swallowed hard before asking, "What's his name?"

"Milo."

Stephen's eyes widened, and he looked back at the boy. "You named him after my grandpa?"

Madison smiled. "Milo was always nice to me. I was sad when he passed away." Madison looked at the picture Stephen held. "As soon as he was born, something about the way his forehead was all scrunched up reminded me of your grandpa. I thought it would be a good name."

Stephen nodded but didn't meet her eyes. She didn't know if he was happy or upset about him. After talking things over with Karen last night, she didn't want to assume too much. She needed to find out why he had never contacted her after she'd tried to find him. And what he wanted to do now that he knew.

Stephen rubbed a finger across the glass. "Can I keep this?" He finally looked up and met her eyes. The hope in them gave her a bit of peace.

"Of course."

Stephen brought the frame closer to him and cradled it in his palms. The sweet motion made her wish he could have held Milo as a baby. He obviously cared, but it had been so long she didn't have a clue where to begin now.

"Can I meet him?" Stephen asked, the hope in his

voice this time was enough to make her sad.

"Yes, but I don't want to move too fast. He doesn't know anything about you."

Stephen frowned. "Nothing?"

Madison tilted her head to the side. "What was I supposed to tell him? His daddy didn't want anything to do with us, and I had no idea where he was?"

"I had no idea. You never called or anything."

Madison's eyes widened in shock, and she struggled to keep the building anger from coming out with her words. "I called your cell phone, and it always went to voicemail. I left messages after the first few times, but you never called back. Your email address you gave me was crap. Kept bouncing back as undeliverable. And no one knew what your physical address was. Your grandparents were gone, and no one in King had contact info for you. We even tried getting ahold of your mom, but nothing. It was obvious after the first six months you didn't care at all, so I gave up."

"That's not true. I cared. I just had something going on and got sidetracked."

"Sidetracked?" Madison repeated, the anger making its way through anyway. "You disappeared and never ever contacted me either. It's been eight years, and my parents are still in King. You could have looked for me." Madison clamped her mouth closed when she realized she'd shouted the last sentence. She knew other people in the restaurant were looking at her, but she didn't look away from Stephen, whose face had darkened into an angry blush under his dark skin. "It doesn't matter now. I didn't need you, and I still don't. But unfortunately, Milo needs to have some sort of contact with his father. He's started asking questions, and I know it's going to get worse the older he gets. So now that you've shown up out of the blue, I might as well let you meet your son."

Stephen kept his mouth shut, and Madison wished he'd say something. When he didn't for another full minute, she shook her head and turned her attention to her sandwich. She took a huge bite, opened her bag of chips, and shoved one in as well. She took a huge swig of her soda and another bite, not looking at Stephen directly. He had turned his attention back to the photograph then carefully tucked it into his suit jacket pocket.

"I'm sorry," he finally whispered, and Madison stopped chewing. "I don't know what else to say. I lost my phone, and when I got it replaced, I got the same number. I should have received those calls. But the week after we got back home, my mom found out she had cancer. She was gone in less than three months."

Madison swallowed the food in her mouth. "Oh no. I'm so sorry."

"Me too. It was a shock and kinda stole away all

my thoughts. I spent as much time with her as I could, and when she was gone, I wasn't ready to face normal. By the time I was ready to carry on again, it was time to move to California. My scholarship wasn't going to allow me to postpone it any longer, so I went."

He looked at Madison, concern and sorrow in his eyes. "I tried to call you, but the phone was always hung up the second they knew who I was. By the time I was ready to return to life and thought about trying to track you down at school, I felt like it had been too long and that you'd have moved on and been dating while at college yourself."

Madison shook her head. "Yeah, I didn't go to college right away."

Stephen reached across the table and hesitantly took her hand in his. "I'm so sorry I wasn't there for you, or Milo. I know I can't change the past, but I'd like to be a part of his future. If you'll let me."

The comfort just his hand brought hers made her wish she could find a way to bottle it up for times when she needed support. He was here now. And she would be careful to guard Milo from disappointment, but Stephen was willing to try, and that was enough.

Chapter Eleven

They'd talked long into the afternoon about Milo. It was hard for Stephen to wrap his mind around the idea of being an instant father. He had no idea what to do with a child, but as he looked at the photograph Madison had brought him, he longed to know the kid. He'd missed seven years of his son's life, and it hurt. He'd thought Madison knew him and understood his past, but when it had come down to it, she had judged him anyway and made the call that he would be an unfit father without giving him a chance to prove her wrong.

He would take things slow, do his best and see where it led, but having his whole existence judged by a kid was intimidating.

Stephen checked his watch again then searched the parking lot for Madison's little car. She'd thought meeting at the park would be a good idea, and as he watched the kids there with their parents, playing on the equipment, he hoped it would go well.

There was five minutes until six, so she wasn't late, but he still worried that she might change her mind. He pulled his phone out and checked to see if she'd sent a message about not coming. His phone was blank, so he put it back in his pocket and studied the parking lot, willing her car to arrive.

He scanned the playground, wondering if this was the best bench to sit on. Should he move over to one closer to the bathrooms? Or was it better to stay on the boundary of the bark-filled play area?

Just as he was about to move over to a different bench, her silver car pulled up. He stood to get a better view of the back seat, hoping to catch a glimpse of Milo, but the booster seat must have been on the other side. As Madison got out of the car and opened the back door for Milo, she searched the playground over the top of her car and seemed to stiffen a little when she saw him.

He made her nervous, and he hated that. They had been such good friends each summer, falling easily into conversation, even with a school year between visits. They never needed to call or write while apart. Perhaps that was why it hadn't seemed odd to him that he hadn't heard from her at first. But after the way their relationship had turned serious at the beginning of that last summer, he should have made a better effort at contacting her.

Two feet jumped out, and Stephen waited impatiently to see the rest of his boy. As Milo moved away from the car, Madison reached for his hand. She shut the door, revealing his child. Finally.

Madison looked down and answered some question Milo had asked then led him toward Stephen, gently reminding him that they would play on the slides and things after meeting her friend.

Milo nodded but looked longingly at the playground. He turned to face Stephen and slowed down just a little. Stephen didn't know if the boy was nervous or just shy. What had Madison told him? He tried to take his eyes off Milo to look at his mother, but it was hard to pull his focus away from his son.

When Madison reached the bench, she bent down close to Milo and looked up at Stephen. "Milo, this is my friend, Stephen."

Stephen's heart sank. She hadn't told him who he was. Just a friend felt like such a slap in the face. He didn't look at Madison, instead focusing on Milo, and the kid smiled.

"Hi." Milo looked at him then back to his mom. "Can I play now?"

"In a second, sweetie. I wanted us to talk to Stephen for a few minutes, then you can go play."

Milo frowned then looked at Stephen. "Do you work with my mom?"

Stephen nodded. "Yes."

"Do you like your job? Mom says it's hard."

Stephen glanced at Madison and smiled. "Yes, I like it, but your mom's right. It is a hard job, but there are fun things too. And your mom is really good at it."

Milo nodded. "Are your kids playing here?" He looked toward the playground at the other children playing, and Stephen sent a panicked look to Madison. She just raised an eyebrow.

"No, I don't have kids playing here right now."

Madison squatted to get closer to her son's eye level. "Do you want to tell him some of the things you like to do, Milo?"

Milo sighed, not taking his eyes off the slide. "I like Legos. Mom wouldn't let me bring any, though. She said I'd lose them."

Stephen smiled. "She's probably right. Legos are easy to get lost. I lost some at the beach once."

"The beach?" Milo asked, turning his face to look up at Stephen. "Which one? I could help you look."

Stephen chuckled. "It was a long time ago. I was just a few years older than you, and I was using my Legos to decorate a sandcastle. Then when it was time to leave, I forgot about them. The next day, the waves had washed away my castle and my Legos with it."

Milo frowned. "That's too bad."

"Yeah, it was pretty sad, so I've been more careful with my Legos ever since then."

"Do you still have Legos?"

Stephen nodded. "Lots of them. I even have some of them on a shelf in my apartment."

"Cool." Milo let go of his mom's hand and moved a few steps closer to Stephen then began explaining the different sets he had and asking Stephen about his. The kid was a chatterbox, but his conversations were way more advanced than Stephen had expected.

"Mom," Milo said, "can I go play at Stephen's house so I can see his Legos?"

Madison smiled but shook her head. "No, probably not. You can go play on the slide now so I can talk to Stephen, but we'll see him again, and you can talk more later."

Milo didn't even say goodbye but rushed over to the playground, happy to finally be free. Stephen watched him go with a mixture of sadness and relief. He turned to Madison, who was still watching her son. "Sorry about that."

"Oh, don't worry. I really enjoyed that conversation. And I wouldn't mind letting him play with my Legos. It's what *friends* do." He couldn't help himself and had to throw that out there.

"Maybe someday." Madison glanced at him. "And

I didn't know how to do this. Friend was the easiest."

He sat down on the bench and motioned for her to join him. "Probably true. And it took a lot of pressure off me, honestly."

"I wasn't ready to tell him you are his dad. I tried coming up with all kinds of ways to bring it up, but I chickened out." Madison's voice went soft.

Stephen took her hand, relieved that she let him. "It's okay. We'll go slow. We've got time, and I don't want to rush things with Milo anyway. I would like to be his friend. Let him get to know me. And when you think the time is right, you can tell him. I'll let you take the lead since you know him."

Madison sighed. "Thank you." She pulled her hand away and wrapped her hands around her purse sitting on her lap as she watched Milo climbing up the slide. "Milo, use it right, please."

Milo stopped climbing and laid on his stomach. He slid down the slide and ran around to the stairs on the opposite side. Stephen was impressed that he followed directions so well without any sort of tantrum. He was a well-mannered child, and Stephen knew his mother had worked hard to teach him that.

"He's a good kid, Madison. You've done really well with him."

Madison glanced at him. "Thanks. I've had help. My sister, Karen, and her husband, Jason, are really good for him. Karen's the one that watches him while I'm at work."

"That's good. It helps to have family support."

Madison nodded but didn't speak.

Stephen watched Milo play, smiling at the imagination just bursting from the kid as he included the other kids on the playground in his game. He had never been that outgoing as a child.

Chapter Twelve

*M*adison took Milo's hand in hers as they walked to the car. Stephen walked on his other side, and she could just imagine him holding Milo's other hand. Instead, they talked about their son's favorite superhero at length. As they reached the car, Milo pulled on the handle to open the door.

Stephen looked at her and the boy as if he didn't want them to leave, but Milo was tired and didn't want to play anymore. As Milo climbed into the car and got settled into his booster seat, Stephen put his hand on the top of the car.

"Would you be interested in going to get some ice cream?"

Madison pressed her lips together to fight the smile that threatened when Milo perked up and started begging. "Please, Mom. Can we go get ice cream?"

"Sure, Milo, but we can't stay long. It's getting

late." She looked at Stephen, not sure how she felt about this impromptu suggestion. "Where did you have in mind?"

Stephen shrugged. "Do you know of a good place for ice cream?" He glanced around as if expecting something close by. "I'm new here."

Madison shook her head slowly. "Silly man."

"We could go get a box of Creamsicles," Stephen suggested.

Madison's mouth watered at the thought. She loved those, and her mom had always bought boxes of them to share during the summers.

"That would be fun." She closed Milo's door. "There is a supermarket a couple blocks away. Would you like to follow me there?"

"Sure." Stephen took a step back then opened her door. "Thank you. For this." He glanced back at the playground then in the back seat at Milo.

"No problem. He had fun. It was a good first meeting."

Stephen nodded but didn't say anything. Madison gave him directions to the supermarket and slid into her car, feeling awkward about having him help her with the door. She lifted her sandaled feet into the car and hesitated to reach for the door, not sure if he would close it or not. She put her key in the ignition, and Stephen closed it and stepped back. She rolled down the window. "Do you want me to wait for you or meet you there?"

Stephen smiled. "I think I can find it. I'll see you there."

Madison waved, and Milo hollered from the back seat, "See you there!"

Stephen waved then turned around to head to his car, and Madison put the car into gear.

"Did you have fun, Milo?" she asked.

"Yeah. I love the park."

"What did you think of my friend?" Madison asked.

"He's really big."

Madison smiled. "Yes, he is."

"Will I get big like him when I'm grown up?"

Madison glanced at him in the rear-view mirror. "Yes, you'll probably get big, just like him."

"I'm gonna be a fireman when I grow up. And if I'm tall like him, I can reach the windows and not need a ladder."

Madison's heart swelled with pride as she listened to Milo talk.

"Would you like to see my friend more?" Madison asked.

"Can we play Legos?" Milo asked. "'Cause I have some I can show him. And he said I could see his."

"I'm sure that could be arranged."

"Do you want to play with the Legos too?" Milo asked. "I will share mine with you. But not my Batman one. Or my pirate ship. But you could use the police station. And since I'll be Batman, I can help you save the city."

He carried on, telling Madison about how the game would go, and she just smiled then wondered how the man would play with him. After watching Stephen climb on the slide and try to fit his broad shoulders through the tube slide, she knew he wasn't afraid to get into a game. He'd been adorable when he acted like the bad guy and had let Milo chase him around the park as the police officer. And though they'd both asked her to join in, she couldn't bring herself to get too close where she wouldn't be able to see it all.

She still wondered if she should have told Milo that Stephen was his father, but she didn't want to ruin this first interaction with a lot of questions. Milo would have been certain to quiz Stephen on where he'd been, and though she had tried not to bad-mouth Stephen, she hadn't been very positive about him when Milo had asked questions.

And now that she understood a little of his reasons for being absent, she felt bad for coloring Milo's perception of his father as someone who didn't care.

For a seven-year-old, he was very intelligent, but she wasn't sure how much he would understand about the whole thing. She still didn't know how she felt about it. She no longer felt the same anger she had about being abandoned, but was still resentful that he had never once tried to look her up.

They'd been each other's firsts, and he was still her only, though she doubted she was his. And though she had dated on occasion, she'd never felt comfortable getting serious with any of the men because of Milo. She didn't want to risk him growing to love some man who would leave them. She kept most dating experiences to just a first date, never wanting to move past that. And the few times she'd let it go to a kiss, she pulled back, not willing to let her heart risk the rejection that might come.

Madison struggled to control her frustration. She had been fine just being Milo's mom and working at Carlson's. She was good at her job, and though it kept her busy, it still allowed her time with Milo. Her sister was her best friend, and she didn't need a man.

But now that Stephen was back in her life, she remembered how much she had loved him. Their relationship had grown over the years, from good friends to much more, and though they'd only been intimate a few times, she'd felt loved and cherished and had known he was the one for her.

Having him disappear had been devastating. Now having him show up threw her emotions into turmoil, and she resented him. If it weren't for Milo, she would do her best to never see the man again, even if it meant finding a different job. Though, if it weren't for Milo, there would be no issue. And she would never give up her son. So she would deal with this the best she could and help her son have a relationship with his father. Even if she never would.

Stephen followed the compact silver car to the supermarket, happy to know he would have a few more minutes with them. Milo was amazing, and he couldn't believe he was connected to the boy. And his mother was even more amazing. Her beauty had just increased over the years. She had filled out in all the right places, and he longed to hold her close, to even just hold her hand, but he had a feeling she wouldn't take to that kindly. He wanted her physically and emotionally, and it hurt that she had shut him out so completely.

Finding her again eight years later had been a fluke, and to have to work with her while trying to sort out how their future might go with Milo in the mix was going to take a lot of work. If only he knew how to go about this whole thing.

He parked his car next to hers, but she got out before he could open her door. She leaned in to help Milo, who had apparently taken off his shoes in the short five-minute drive.

"Leave your shoes on next time, kiddo."

"I hate these shoes. They hurt my feet," Milo complained. "I have a blister now."

"Well, then let me know before we leave the house so we can get the right size." Madison slipped his shoes back on him and pressed the Velcro strap down. She stepped back to let him climb out, but he stood inside the car and reached his hands out.

"Carry me."

"You can walk."

"I don't wanna walk. My feet are hurt," Milo said.

Before Madison could say no again, Stephen spoke. "I could carry him."

Madison turned to him with a surprised look and Milo eagerly squealed. "Yay!"

He put his arms out, and Stephen stepped forward, brushing his arm against Madison as she moved to the side. He turned around and squatted low so Milo could climb on his back. He put his hands under Milo's legs and lifted him carefully out of the car, not sure how much force to put in the movement.

Milo was a solid kid, and though not overly heavy,

Stephen knew why Madison had been hesitant to carry him. Milo wrapped his little legs around Stephen's waist as if he knew exactly where to sit, but Stephen still struggled for a moment before adjusting him to the right place where he could walk without feeling as if he'd drop the kid or have his feet hitting his legs as he moved.

"Thanks," Milo said, and Stephen smiled.

Madison didn't say anything but lifted her purse higher onto her shoulder then closed the car door and walked to the supermarket. She led the way, heading directly to the frozen section and stopping in front of the ice cream. This store was familiar to her, so he figured she must live close by. He was only five miles away, which was good. It would allow him to see them more often.

"Which kind?" Madison asked.

"I vote Creamsicle," Stephen said.

"Me too," Milo agreed then looked at the selection. "What are Creamsicles?"

Stephen chuckled then pointed at the box with vanilla ice cream coated in orange Popsicle. "Only the best ice cream out there."

Milo leaned closer to the glass door and studied the box. "Can I have it?" He looked at his mom, and she nodded. "Okay. I'll try it."

"Good boy," Stephen said and held up his fist for

a knuckle bump.

Milo pushed his fist against Stephen's then pulled it back and wiggled his fingers, making Stephen chuckle again.

Madison opened the freezer and pulled out the box then headed to the checkout line. Stephen followed closely and pulled out his wallet. He slid his debit card out and, when the cashier rang it up, he stepped forward. "I've got this. My treat."

Madison seemed to hesitate for a minute then stepped back and let him scan the card. He was glad she hadn't put up a fight. She pulled the box out of the bag and smiled at the cashier. "We won't need the bag."

Stephen took the receipt and handed it to her so she could walk out with the ice cream.

Stephen saw a woman struggling to pull a shopping cart free from the train of carts shoved together as she held one small kid on her hip. A car seat rested on the crook of her other arm. He moved over to help her, and when the buckle that was holding the carts together was untangled, he pulled the cart free and helped her lift the car seat onto the cart.

"Thank you." She looked at Milo. "You've got a good daddy there."

Milo looked at Stephen as the lady walked away. "Are you a good daddy?"

Stephen's gut tightened. He hadn't been so far. "I hope so, Milo. I really do." Madison was too far ahead to have overheard, for which he was thankful.

He helped Milo get into the car and watched as the kid buckled himself in. "Can I have the ice cream now?" He held his hand out, but Madison shook her head.

"No ice cream in the car. We can go back to the park and eat it."

Milo frowned. "But it will melt. The park is too far away."

Madison shook her head. "It will be fine."

Stephen wondered why they hadn't just carpooled if they were returning to the park, but he kept quiet, not wanting to ask. He opened Madison's door, but when Milo spoke from the back seat for them to hurry so it didn't melt, he let her close it and moved over to his car. Minutes later, they were sitting under a tree on the grass, and Madison unwrapped the ice cream then handed it to Milo. She passed the box over to Stephen, so he got two out, opened one, and passed it to her stick first.

She met his eyes, smiled, and reached for it. When her fingers brushed his, she looked down at his hands then kept her eyes on the ice cream, not looking at him again.

It was probably a good thing, because the simple

brush of her hand against his had sent shivers up his arm and straight into his chest, making it slightly difficult to breathe. He unwrapped his Creamsicle then took a bite and watched Milo as he tried the ice cream. He started licking it, but Stephen shook his head.

"You should bite it. The ice cream is underneath."

Milo looked at his mom, and she nodded, so Milo took a bite, shivered, then smiled. "This is good."

Chapter Thirteen

*M*adison watched as Milo and Stephen talked and talked. Stephen told him about the things he'd done as a kid in Hawaii, and Milo asked about the ocean and if it was the same as the one at his beach.

"The water is a lot like here. But there's one beach I used to go to that had black sand."

"Black?" Milo asked. "Was it dirty?"

Stephen chuckled. "No, it was because of a volcano. The sand is made of little pieces of broken lava."

"Is it hot?" Milo asked.

"Not from the volcano, since it's really old. But sometimes if the sun shines on it too much, it gets hot." Stephen leaned back, using his arms to brace himself. "Hawaii has a lot of really neat beaches."

Milo turned to Madison. "Will we ever go to

Hawaii?"

"Maybe someday," she said.

Milo looked at Stephen. "My dad lives in Hawaii. Mom said I look like him."

Madison's heart stopped for a moment. She had told him that once, when he had asked over a year ago, and she hadn't realized he'd remembered it. She looked at Stephen who was silent but staring at her. She took a slow breath and scooted closer to Milo, which in turn put her closer to Stephen, making her more nervous than she liked.

"Milo, sweetie, I need to tell you something."

Milo looked at her, and she saw the sticky remains of his second ice cream around his lips. She reached in her bag for a wet wipe, needing just a moment to prepare herself. Milo rolled his eyes but allowed her to clean him up. She leaned closer and stared into his deep brown eyes that looked so much like the brown eyes she felt boring into her back.

"Milo, my friend Stephen is your daddy."

Milo looked at Stephen with wide eyes then a huge grin spread across his face. "You're my dad?"

Stephen nodded slowly then glanced at Madison then back to Milo. "Yes. I'm sorry I haven't been here before."

"Are you going to start living at our house like Uncle Jason lives at Aunt Karen's house?"

Madison's face flamed, and she refused to look at Stephen. "No, sweetie, he won't be living with us. But I want you guys to know each other, so you'll see him a lot."

"Okay," Milo said. "And will you let me play with your Legos?" The seriousness of his question made Madison almost giggle.

"Sure, Milo. We could play with them," Stephen said. He looked at Madison and she met his eyes, not sure how he would feel about her sudden revelation to Milo. He just looked at her then turned his attention back to Milo as the boy asked question after question about Hawaii, then more questions about when they could see the Legos.

She listened again, relieved to know Milo accepted the news without any stress or awkward questions about where he'd been and why he hadn't been with them before. Of course, to a seven-year-old, those things wouldn't really matter much.

Her emotions warred with each other. No one else had been as important in Milo's life as she had been, even Karen and Jason had been second fiddle to her. But Milo seemed to be opening his little soul to this stranger he had only just met and was already considering him important, just because he had the title of father.

Guilt pricked at her as she wished Stephen had

stayed absent, but as she saw how much Milo enjoyed asking questions about his father to his actual father, the anger and betrayal at Stephen's absence began to wash away. He could be a part of Milo's life without taking away from her.

Madison played with the sticks from the Creamsicles and watched the two as they caught up. When she glanced at her watch, she reluctantly interrupted.

"It's about time to head home, buddy."

"Just ten more minutes?" Milo asked.

Stephen smiled and Madison joined him.

"How about five? Then we need to go so you can have a bath tonight."

Milo moaned. "I hate baths." He turned to look at Stephen. "Want to slide with me for five minutes?"

Madison shook her head. "I need to talk to him for a few minutes. How about you run slide while we figure out a time for you to meet again?"

"Okay," Milo said and ran off to the playground, his blister completely forgotten.

"Sorry about that," Madison said.

"I didn't want to slide anyway," Stephen said then winked.

"No, I mean for dumping it like that, and then for him going nonstop. I guess I should have prepared him for this better."

Stephen shook his head. "No, it was fine. I enjoyed it. It felt kinda natural, and he had a right to ask lots of questions."

Madison nodded thoughtfully as she watched Milo climb the ladder. She glanced at Stephen from the corner of her eye to see him watching their son as well. "How are we going to go about this?"

"Well, apparently you're not ready for me to move in."

Madison whipped her head around to gawk at him.

"I'm joking." He grinned, and she eased a little. "I think we should go slow. But I'd like to see him as often as you'll let me. I'd like to try to be a good dad for him."

Madison nodded. Of course he'd want to be a part of Milo's life. And though she didn't want him as a lover or anything, it still hurt that he didn't seem to be interested in her now, just in their son. Of course, that was how it should be. It had been too long ago to try to go back to the connection they'd had. And she'd grown up since then and knew that it had just been a teenage infatuation. There was nothing lasting about their time together. Why should she hope there would be something now?

"I don't want to come to the park every day," Madison said. "And I'm not ready for him to go with you alone. But we could meet here a couple times a week then maybe go for a walk or out to McDonald's or something once in a while."

"That sounds good," Stephen said. "Can I pick you two up for dinner tomorrow?"

Madison turned to him. "How about we meet you there?"

He hesitated for a minute, and she wondered if he knew she didn't want to let him know where she lived. She wasn't ready for him to show up at her door. But why she was so hesitant, she didn't know. She hated feeling so conflicted with him. She used to be so in control of everything, but after seeing him in Mr. Carlson's office, things had been so out of whack, and she hated it.

They made plans for where to meet, and Madison called Milo to join her. They left the park together, and Stephen once again opened her door and helped her in. He leaned down to wave to Milo. "See you tomorrow."

"Bye, Dad."

Madison's heart froze. Milo had taken to him immediately and, without any prompting or hesitance whatsoever, had completely accepted him as his father.

She glanced at Stephen to see if he'd been affected by it at all and frowned to see the shock and surprise in his face.

Oh, Milo would sure make this interesting. Question was, could she survive it?

Chapter Fourteen

*M*adison opened the door to her office, surprised to see a bouquet of flowers on her desk. She smiled at the variety of colors, all of the same flower. Snapdragons. Her favorite growing up. Her mother had a huge flower garden reserved just for snapdragons, and Madison and her sisters had always pulled off the petals and pinched the corners to make the mouth open.

She looked for a card and wasn't surprised to see it was from Stephen. It only said a simple *Thank you*, but she smiled anyway. Nothing romantic, which was good, but the flowers were a sweet reminder of their childhood. They had had some good times each summer, and she let herself remember them for a moment. She rubbed her fingers across the soft lips of one flower, then not even hesitating, she pulled it from the stem and pinched the corners just like she used to do at home.

As the mouth opened, she smiled as she thought of what the flowers would have to say. She squeezed it a couple times making the mouth open and close. Just before she began speaking for it, a knock on her door made her turn around. Stephen stood there, a soft smile on his face. She lifted the flower petal up and pressed the lips. "Thank you."

He smiled wider and stepped inside. "You're welcome. Thanks for letting me meet Milo. Would it be okay if I gave him something today?" He took another step toward her but stopped and fidgeted with his hands. "Something to make up for all the birthdays I missed."

Madison raised her eyebrow. "Like what?"

"A Lego set?" Stephen smiled. "I found one he said he didn't have and wanted to save up for."

Madison thought for a moment, wondering if that would give Milo the wrong impression, that he would be getting gifts from Stephen all the time. Or did Stephen think he needed to buy his way into Milo's affections? "I'm not sure if that's a good idea."

Stephen's smile disappeared. "Do you mind telling me why?"

Madison rubbed her finger across the petal of the snapdragon she still held. "Well, because you just met, and I don't want him to think you'll be bringing him toys all the time. It's not his birthday and I've tried to be careful to not make him think he can have whatever he wants. He's been saving his money for that, and if you just give it to him, he won't learn anything. Besides, Lego sets are huge and expensive, and I don't think that will set a good precedent for your interactions with each other."

Stephen nodded slowly, but she could tell he didn't agree with her. "What about a smaller set then? I can save this one for his birthday later." He tilted his head to the side. "When is his birthday anyway?"

"May 4th."

Stephen grinned. "He's a *Star Wars* baby?"

Madison furrowed her brow. "A what?"

"*Star Wars*. May the fourth. May the fourth be with you?"

Madison chuckled. "I've never heard of that."

"You've seen *Star Wars*. I know you have. We watched it together."

Stephen smiled, and Madison nodded. From what she could remember, they'd made out a lot during those movies though, so was it any wonder she hadn't paid much attention to the show?

"I think saving the big set for a birthday would be better, if you don't mind. The smaller one would be fine, but I don't want you to buy him stuff all the time. He has lots of toys, and he doesn't need you to buy your way into his life."

Stephen frowned. "I wasn't trying to buy my way in. I just wanted to do something nice for him."

Madison nodded. "I know. This is just really new to me, and I'm not sure how to deal with it all."

Stephen glanced at the clock on her wall. "Are we still planning on meeting at three to go over the proposal?"

"Yes." Madison was glad he'd changed the subject. Trying to keep their personal life — or whatever this was — between them and their professional life separate was hard. "I've just about finished the presentation from the notes you gave me. I think I can get them done before then." She dropped the flower petal into the trash on her way around her desk. Then looked back at Stephen. "I'll see you at three then."

He nodded and left her alone in the office with his flowers and too many memories of that last summer echoing in her mind. She picked another petal, fresher and squeezable again. "May the fourth," she whispered as she moved the flower's lips. "Too funny."

Stephen left her office more confused than ever.

She seemed to like the flowers, and he was glad, but why couldn't he give his child a present? It wasn't as if he planned to spoil the kid. He had missed seven years of his life and felt like he owed Milo something for that. But he supposed she was right. And Madison knew him best. If he wanted to be a part of Milo's life, he'd have to do it on her terms.

He probably had some sort of parental rights, but if he tried fighting for them, she would dig in her heels, and he'd ruin any chance of having her support him in the relationship with his child. Besides, a part of him wanted to see if he could possibly pursue a relationship with Madison.

The more he saw her, the more he wanted to get to know her again. They had been such good friends, and though having sex had changed things between them, in a bigger way than just becoming parents, he'd been gone so soon after they reached that stage that he was sure she had lost all feelings for him. And getting her to give him a chance now would be much harder than starting a relationship with a stranger.

He had their past mistakes to overcome as well as navigating this new parental aspect. He vowed to do his best to make things right with them, and if he could make her fall in love with him again, that would be the best option out there. Going about it too strong would backfire. He would have to work at it through his relationship with Milo and keep things professional here at work.

He squared his shoulders as he walked back to his office. He could do this.

When three o'clock rolled around, he knocked on Madison's office door. She waved him in while still talking on the phone. He brought his chair around to the other side of her desk as she continued her conversation, and he opened his laptop to get things ready.

Her small dish with chocolates was empty, and he frowned. He didn't really need the candy, but it had become a habit, and he missed it. He knew there had been a bunch earlier. He'd seen them when he'd talked to her that morning. Had she eaten them all?

He pushed the thought out of his mind when she finished her call and turned to him. As they talked about the presentation and the upcoming schedule, he reflected on how good she was at her job. It was a pleasure to work with her, but the more he watched her and the closer they worked together, the more he longed to reach out and take her hand.

She wouldn't appreciate that though, so he turned his attention back to the project, and they finished it in record time.

"I think the pitch will go really well. Mr. Carlson will have another client signed soon," Stephen said.

"I hope so," Madison said as she closed the program down. She yawned and wiped her eyes. "Sorry. Didn't sleep much last night."

"Too much on your mind?"

She nodded. "Yeah, and Milo couldn't stop talking. I think he had a great time yesterday. Thank you for that. You handled it really well."

Stephen smiled. "I enjoyed it. He's a good kid." He reached for her hand and was relieved she let him take it. "Thank you for doing such a good job with him. He's lucky to have you as his mother."

Madison nodded and didn't speak. He released her hand, not wanting to force himself on her or make her pull away from him because she felt pressured. "Are we still meeting tonight for dinner?" he asked.

"Yes, Milo's excited."

Well, at least that was a start. Of course, Madison probably wasn't all that excited about going to eat at a fast food restaurant with an indoor play land. He would have to ask her out to dinner, just the two of them. If she'd accept.

He hoped she would.

"I'll see you there, then." Stephen stood and walked toward the door of her office.

Madison watched him leave and opened her top drawer to get out her stash of chocolates she'd hidden. It had been silly, but she'd loved seeing him search the bowl for a treat to steal and find nothing there. She'd make sure the bowl was full again tomorrow, but having that little bit of control again helped her feel at peace. She peeled the wrapper of the Butterfinger and popped it in her mouth as she prepared to leave for the day.

Though work was over, she wished she could stay there since leaving meant she had to take Milo and herself to eat with Stephen. Milo was excited because they rarely went out for dinner as it was much cheaper to cook at home. And for them to go to one with a play land was even better. It felt like such a splurge, and she worried Milo would think Stephen was cool just because he could buy him things.

But would Stephen be an actual parent and set rules and consequences, or would he be all for the fun and bend the rules? He'd been that way as a kid, getting into trouble and sweet-talking his way out. It was no surprise he was so good in marketing. He could sell anything and convince you to see his way.

She would have to be firm and make sure he understood his role with Milo wouldn't be all fun and games. He needed a father figure, not just a big boy at a playdate.

Chapter Fifteen

he next few days moved smoothly. Milo and Madison had seen him each day, and Stephen thought he was making progress in the fatherhood department. But he couldn't crack Madison's shell at work.

She was very professional, and they worked well together, bringing in two more accounts with a couple more being very likely to sign within the next few weeks. They had met for lunch once, and when he'd tried to offer to buy her meal, she'd refused. But they had discussed Milo more than business, so she wouldn't let him write it off as a business lunch either.

He'd learned so much about Milo over the last few days that he felt he was beginning to know the kid. And Milo had expressed interest in coming to Stephen's home more than once, but Madison had said no. Yet she still refused to let him come to her house. They always met in public areas in separate vehicles where she could leave on her own terms.

Stephen pushed his rolling chair away from his desk and slid it over to look out the large window lining his wall. Looking down over the city had always helped him clear his mind before, but now he just thought it looked too jumbled and messy. He never thought he'd long for it, but seeing all the building, traffic, and pollution, a small part of him wished he could look out over his grandpa's fields from the front porch. The same place he'd stood countless times watching for signs of Bea's family to come back in from checking the cattle out on their grazing lands so he'd know if it was worth starting the beat-up old truck to head over to see her.

He closed his eyes and tried visualizing the serenity of King, Montana, but fell short with the sounds of the air conditioning unit on. He took a slow breath then moved back to his desk to finish the project. A knock on his open door brought his head up, and he blinked in surprise at the woman standing at the door. He'd never seen her in the office, but she looked like she belonged here.

"Are you Mr. Kohalohini?" She struggled over the name just a little but not bad.

"I am." Stephen stood up and approached her.

"I'm Carrie." She offered her hand. "Mr. Carlson

asked me to check and see if there was anything you'd like help on. Madison called in sick today."

Stephen wondered if Madison was all right. Hopefully, it wasn't serious. She had seemed fine last night, but Milo had been a little quieter than usual. Maybe she was taking a sick day on the boy's account. He pulled himself out of his wonder about Madison and looked at Carrie. "I think I'll be fine. We aren't pitching to anyone until next week, and I believe we're on top of things for the moment."

Carrie smiled. "Excellent. I've been helping Madison on some of the accounts, so if you have any questions later, let me know."

She turned away then glanced over her shoulder, giving him a quick once-over, and smiled again as she walked back to her office. He couldn't help following her with his gaze as she left. She was beautiful and friendly, but he didn't get the same desire to pursue her he would have just months ago. Now it was only Madison who filled his thoughts.

Stephen texted her quickly to see if she was okay and see if there was anything he could do.

Stomach bug. We'll have to reschedule Milo's meet-up with you.

Is he sick too? Stephen asked.

Yeah.

I'll bring soup tonight. Gimme your addy, or I'll get it from the files here.

No need. I've got soup.

Madison's response made him shake his head, even though she couldn't see.

Not my special recipe. It's a cure-all. Grandma Iris taught me.

Madison's response to that made him smile.

You've got Iris's secret soup recipe?

Yup, and if you just tell me your addy, I'll bring some by tonight. You know you want it. It's a miracle cure.

Stephen stared at the phone, willing the next text to give the address.

You win.

Her response brought a whoop from him. That text was soon followed by her address and instructions how to get there.

But you can't stay long. Don't want to pass this on to you.

Understood. Get some rest, I'll be over around 7:00.

He turned back to his desk and pulled open the files. After going over one of the proposals, he smiled at how thorough Madison had been on their plan. He made a few phone calls and sent a few emails then did some research on the latest marketing trends to keep abreast of them. When the knock came again on his open door, he looked up and smiled wide to see Carrie standing there again.

"I was about to head to lunch. You want me to

pick you up something?"

Stephen checked his clock and stood to stretch. "I hadn't even noticed what time it was. That's nice of you, but I brought something from home."

Carrie's smile slipped a little, but she nodded and turned to leave. Stephen wondered if he should work through lunch so he could leave early and stop by the supermarket to get the ingredients for the soup. His stomach rumbled at the thought of food. Maybe he could heat it up and eat it while working. That way he could come to Madison's aide much sooner.

Madison curled over the bowl, hoping the urge to vomit would pass. She'd spent half the night trying to clean up all the pukes from Milo, who hadn't made it to the bathroom the first time. At least now, he was resting on the couch surrounded by towels and blankets with a bowl in his hand to catch anything else.

She had worried at first that it was a reaction to some nut contamination in something he'd eaten, but he hadn't shown any other signs typical of his food allergy. He hadn't thrown up for a couple hours, but he had a mild fever and complained of aching. She hoped her bout with the stomach bug would pass as quickly. When she called Karen to let her know they were staying home sick, Karen said they'd come down with something as well.

Every time she'd had to deal with a sick child on her own through the night, she had longed for the companionship of a husband to help her. To take over when she couldn't do it anymore. Now that Stephen was back in her life, she wondered if she should possibly give him a chance with her. Not just see how he did with Milo, but to see if maybe there was any chance the two of them could work things out. The fact that he'd checked on her and was going to bring Iris's delicious soup made her heart thaw toward him just a little more. She touched the cell phone sitting on the armrest of the loveseat, thinking how sweet it was he'd offered to help.

Madison looked around the little house and the mess it was in after this sickness. She would have to clean it up before he got there. When she stood up, a wave of dizziness washed over her, and she sat back down and leaned her head against the back of the seat. It would have to wait. Besides, she had a few hours.

Chapter Sixteen

*M*adison dozed throughout the afternoon, subsisting on crackers and apple juice and a few ibuprofen. The stomach bug had come and gone, but her body still hurt, and she just wanted to take a long hot bath to soothe her aching joints. She looked at the clock, and figured she'd have time to bathe before Stephen arrived in an hour.

She grabbed her blanket, scattered tissues, and the cracker box, then checked on Milo.

"How you feeling, buddy?"

"Better." Milo looked up from the video game he'd been playing quietly on the couch. He still looked pale, and his eyes weren't as bright as usual, but he did look improved from the morning.

"Good. I'm going to take a bath. Stephen said he'd bring us some soup in about an hour. You be good."

"Kay." Milo's eyes trailed back to the TV screen,

and she headed to her bath.

Madison turned on the playlist on her phone and set it on the counter. She poured in some of her bath salts, the fragrant ones she saved for special occasions, and slid into the hot water, sighing at the way her muscles relaxed. If only there was some way to bottle up that sensation. The music, combined with the warm water made her drift off to sleep, and she woke with a start when her head tilted to the side and water filled her ears.

The water was still warm enough to remain for a few minutes longer, so she slipped under the water, submersing her head; she rubbed her scalp, enjoying the sensations that brought. Knowing she should get out soon, she pulled the plug and turned on the shower to rinse off, then reached out for her towel.

She lathered herself in her favorite body lotion, and combed through her hair then let it hang down her back. She didn't want to bother blowing it dry. She looked for her change of clothes and realized she hadn't grabbed a set or her robe. Not wanting to put her dirty clothes back on, she tossed them into the hamper, wrapped the towel around her body and tucked the corner in to hold it like a sarong.

It didn't go down her thighs very far, but it was still long enough to cover her butt. And Milo wouldn't even notice; he'd probably still have his eyes glued to the television. She checked the clock. It was six-thirty, so she knew she should hurry and get dressed before Stephen came over with the soup.

She opened the door, and the sounds of Milo's game reached her ears. She headed toward the front room. "Milo, it's time to turn that off and do a tidy up if you—" Her words fell right out of her mouth as she met Stephen's big brown eyes. She froze and stared at him.

Stephen sat next to Milo on the couch, the game controller forgotten in his hands as he stared at Madison. The towel covered her just as much as some dresses he'd seen on women, but his face flushed at the idea of nothing there besides that bit of terrycloth fabric. She brought her hands up to the edge of the towel and pulled it up just a little, but that only brought his attention to her full figure, and he struggled to keep his eyes on her face and not let it roam over her body.

Madison didn't walk away, just stared at him, and though he wanted to speak, he couldn't think of a thing to say. At least nothing that wouldn't get him in trouble.

"Oh, Mom, Stephen brought the soup."

Madison seemed to struggle to take her eyes off him, giving Stephen a jolt of hope. He smiled and glanced at Milo, hoping to give her time to come to grips with his presence there. "I got off a little early and started the soup, then thought I'd bring it over to help you get better sooner."

Milo pointed at the kitchen. "It's on the stovetop. He wanted to keep it warm for you."

Madison nodded numbly then turned without a word and disappeared back down the hallway. He stared at the place she'd stood, not able to get the image of her beauty out of his mind. Seeing her like that definitely solidified his desire to rekindle that flame they'd once shared. And she hadn't gotten angry at him, hadn't yelled and told him to leave, hadn't over reacted at being caught in a towel in the privacy of her own home.

This soup idea was paying untold benefits. He only hoped it was actually as good as what Grandma Iris had always made. Stephen turned to Milo. "Maybe we should turn this off and do the tidy-up she was talking about." He looked around the room, trying to figure out what needed to be done, but it looked pretty good to him.

Milo sighed but shut the game off, put the controllers away, then grabbed his blanket and folded it before placing it in a basket next to the couch.

Stephen looked toward the kitchen with the little table in a breakfast nook. "Should I set the table?"

Milo nodded. "Yeah."

Stephen went back into the kitchen and checked the soup; he turned the temperature off and placed the hot pad he'd brought with him on the table. He examined the closed cupboards and made a guess to which one housed the dishes. He guessed wrong on the first try but found the bowls on the second and set three at the table. He hoped she'd let him stay and decided he'd fare better if he played it cool and just put them all on and had it ready for when she came out.

He looked up after placing the last spoon near the bowl to find Madison watching him. He smiled and turned to face her. "I'm sorry about the early arrival. I should have called first."

Madison shrugged. "No harm done." She looked at the table, her gaze resting on the pot. She took a slow breath and smiled. "Smells amazing. Thank you."

Stephen motioned for her to sit down and called for Milo to join them. He came in and slid onto his seat, then Stephen sat down. He was glad there were four chairs around the table instead of just two. Stephen met Madison's eyes, and she smiled then spoke. "Would you like to offer a blessing on the food?"

Stephen blinked in surprise, not used to doing that

on his own, but it had been a tradition in his grandparent's house, even though it wasn't at his own. He paused for a moment, wondering what to say, then decided to just speak his heart and let the words come as they would.

When he finished, Madison met his eyes again but didn't speak. He looked away from her and used the ladle to dish her up some soup, filled Milo's bowl, and then his own. Milo paused for a minute, looked at his mom and back to Stephen. "Does this have any nuts in it?"

Stephen shook his head. "No."

Madison studied the bowl in front of her. "Does it have anything that could have been processed with nuts?" She turned to Stephen.

He smiled. "I can just give you the recipe. You don't need to go about it this way." Madison opened her mouth to respond, but he kept going. "I know, he's got a nut allergy, but I don't think there is anything that contained nuts, but if you'd like I can tell you all the ingredients."

She took a slow breath and sighed. "What do you think, Milo? Do you trust him?"

For a second, Stephen worried she was serious, then the twinkle in her eye as she glanced at him while Milo mulled it over made him smile.

"Yeah, he's good." Milo lifted his spoon, blew on

the soup, and took a sip. He put the spoon down inside the dish, then his eyes widened, and he grabbed his throat. Stephen dropped his spoon back into his bowl and leaned forward, panicked that he'd added something wrong. Milo stuck his tongue out, rolled his eyes to the back of his head, and dropped his head to the side, making a theatrical croaking sound.

Madison giggled, and Stephen leaned back, shaking his head. "That was mean."

Milo grinned. "Sorry, Dad. But you should have seen your face."

Stephen froze at the use of the word Dad. It sounded so strange to his ears, but he loved it, feeling such a strange mix of emotions. He was terrified he'd do something wrong and mess up any chances he had with these two, but to know Milo had accepted him and didn't hold his absence against him was amazing.

Stephen turned to Madison, who had focused on her soup. She took a slow bite, savoring the flavors, and sighed. "Well, Mr. Kohalohini, I think you might almost be as good as your grandma with this soup."

Stephen smiled and took a spoonful as well. It wasn't anything huge — it wasn't even fancy — but Stephen loved this moment and hoped there would be a lot more of them.

Chapter Seventeen

*M*adison finally felt well enough Saturday morning to venture out to the store for a few supplies. As she wandered the store aisles with Milo beside her, she wondered about getting something nice to cook for when she invited Stephen over for dinner. He was a good cook, at least with the soup, so she'd have to think of something impressive.

"Hey, buddy, what do you say we invite Stephen over for dinner next week?"

Milo lit up just like she'd expected him to. They discussed the different types of meals that Milo liked and tried to come up with one that they thought would be good for Stephen.

"Can we make cupcakes too? Stephen said he liked those," Milo said. It sounded strange for him to call his father by his first name, but she preferred it over the times he'd used Dad. Stephen had said he was fine with it and would let Milo call him what felt comfortable for the boy, and that made her appreciate him even more.

"Yeah, cupcakes sound great. And I think I remember his favorite flavor was chocolate." Madison smiled at Milo's toothless grin since he'd recently lost another one of his front teeth. "Let's go see what we can find."

The more she thought about inviting him over for dinner, the more excited she got, and the butterflies in her stomach told her maybe she would enjoy it as much as Milo would. She couldn't wait until Monday to see him at work. She'd invite him in person instead of a text.

On Monday morning, Madison took extra care in getting ready for work. She made sure her skirt and blouse were attractive but not too provocative. As she dropped Milo off at her sister's, Karen caught her excitement and asked about it.

"I'm just feeling a little hopeful today. Milo and I decided we'd invite Stephen over for dinner." Her cheeks hurt from the grin that wouldn't go away.

Karen studied Madison and smiled. "Good for you. Take a step forward. From everything Milo's said about him, he sounds great. And you've not had anything bad to say about him for a while now."

Madison nodded. "He's really good with Milo. I

can actually say I'm glad he's part of his life now."

Karen hugged her quickly, and Madison rushed back to her car. She wanted to get to work a bit early to make sure everything was running smoothly so she could focus on the right time to ask him for dinner. She knew Carrie had been covering for her on the accounts since Robert hadn't been able to do them from home, like Mr. Carlson had hoped. Carrie was good, and Madison wasn't worried about finding a mess to clean up. In fact, she hoped she might convince Carrie to take over the accounts for good so she could start working more with Stephen to bring in new clients. She'd discovered she was pretty good at it and working with someone of his talents made it even better. If she was lucky, maybe she could convince Mr. Carlson to let her stay in the new client manager position even after Robert returned.

Inside her office, she restocked her candy dish, generously putting a couple extra Butterfingers on top. She opened her laptop and started reviewing the files and customer accounts. Everything looked to be up to date, and there were only a few notes in the accounts from Carrie on things that Madison would need to finish up. It was such a relief to come back after being sick and not have a mountain of work.

Carrie knocked on her door as she entered. "Hey, Madison. Good to see you're back. Are you feeling better?"

Madison smiled. "Yes, much better, thanks." She pointed at the computer. "You did awesome. Thanks for taking care of this."

"No worries. I just wanted to make sure you were here and find out if you needed me to do anything, or if you had questions about things from when you were gone."

Madison shook her head. "No, the notes in here are perfect. I'll take care of those last few things and get these other accounts in progress."

Carrie nodded. "'Kay, let me know if you have questions later." She turned to walk out the door, and Madison watched her leave through the glass walls, thankful for a co-worker who was so helpful.

She turned her head down toward her laptop, but from the corner of her eye, she saw Stephen's large frame and looked back up, excited to see him. Before he reached her door, he raised his eyes to look at Carrie who'd turned around and moved back to join him.

"Anything you need help on this week?" Carrie asked.

Stephen shook his head. "Can't think of anything. Now that Madison's back, we'll pick up where we left off and get the proposal ready."

He turned to Madison's door and walked in, not bothering to knock this time, probably since she was watching him.

"Hey, Madison. Good to see you back." He moved into the office and picked up a candy.

Madison smiled smugly.

"Looks like Grandma's soup did the trick."

Madison nodded. "Thanks. It was just as good as I remember it."

Stephen smiled. "I've got skills." He blew on his fingers and rubbed them on his chest. "You up for meeting at three still? We'll go over the pitch for this Wednesday."

She nodded and swallowed. "Sure. Three's good." She looked at her laptop. "I have a few things to take care of, but Carrie was thorough while I was gone."

"Carrie's pretty impressive." Stephen glanced behind him toward the door. "Mr. Carlson has a great staff here. I'll be sad to leave it when the time comes."

Madison frowned at the reminder. Of course he planned on leaving still. "I've got to make some phone calls. I'll see you at three."

Stephen nodded and grabbed another Butterfinger before walking out of her office.

Chapter Eighteen

When Stephen reached Madison's door at three, he paused before knocking. Her shoulders were slumped, and she stared at the picture of Milo as if not really focused. She looked up and caught him watching her. Madison's expression went from lost in thought to surprise to what he hoped wasn't actually sadness.

Every time she looked at him, he felt like she only remembered the bad things. He needed to find a way to bring out the good or at least distract her from her memories. "So tell me what your thoughts are for the Sharston account."

Madison blinked a few times then looked down at her laptop then back up at him. "I hadn't really planned much more than what we'd discussed last week."

Stephen nodded. "It's a great start, but I was kinda busy this past week working on another potential client and didn't think much on it myself either. Maybe we should build off what you've started."

He placed his laptop on the desk and left it closed, forcing her to pull up all the files she had. She could do this one on her own. And though his ideas on this one would have been good, he knew he could steer her toward them as they worked.

Madison kept her attention on her laptop, rarely even glancing at him, and though the constant rejection kind of stung, he knew it was for the best. He wouldn't force himself on her anymore. And being the good person she was, she would still let him be a part of Milo's life. For that he would be forever grateful.

Yet as she worked and they discussed the pitch, the easy way they had of talking came back. She became animated as he complimented her on her ideas, and she seemed to open up again. He met her eyes, and when she gave him a genuine smile, he felt his heart knot just a little.

She would be the end of him one way or another.

Madison couldn't believe how easy and comfortable the afternoon with Stephen had gone. They'd finalized the proposal for the Sharston account, and he'd never once shot down one of her ideas. Sure, he'd tweaked them a little, adding some of his own flair, but this proposal would come mostly from her.

He'd been close enough for the last hour that she had become used to his cologne, but every once in a while, he would move a little, and a whiff of the masculine scent would surprise her. She longed to lean against him and see if it was on his shirt or only on his neck. She could feel the warmth of his skin even though they weren't touching, and it was driving her crazy.

As a teen, she would have done anything to touch him, lightly brush up against him, slide her chair closer, playfully push his arm; but here in the office, she didn't feel right about that. And she'd gone so long holding back any kind of physical desire. At first she hadn't wanted anyone but Stephen; then after Milo was born, and she was responsible for all his needs and constantly touched by the infant, she didn't think being touched by anyone else would ever be welcome. But now she longed for the comforting touch of another human.

Someone not her family.

Someone who could hold her softly, gently, yet make her ache with longing and then help fill that need. She glanced out of the corner of her eye at Stephen and turned her head to find him watching her as well.

As their eyes met, Stephen leaned closer, and

130

Madison felt herself moving toward him. He lifted his hand to push her hair behind her ear. She held still, allowing the touch of his fingers to slide gently over her skin, then he brushed his fingers across her jawline.

Shivers went down her right side all the way to her toes. His hand rested against her cheek, and she leaned into it, reveling in the comfort it gave. He didn't pull his hand back, but she slowly straightened her head and met his eyes. The openness of his expression was enough to startle her. Had she read his interaction with Carrie wrong? Could he possibly find her attractive? Madison closed her eyes, shaking her head slightly in disbelief, then immediately opened them when he pulled his hand away.

He must have come to his senses because he lowered his hand and cleared his throat. Madison adjusted her shirt, even though there was nothing wrong with it, besides the fact it gave her something to do.

Stephen cleared his throat. "You've got a great pitch outlined here. I think we could go over it just before the meeting Wednesday, unless you'd like to meet again tomorrow at three."

Madison couldn't tell what he wanted, but with the way he'd pulled back and the way she was reeling from what had almost happened — or what she wanted to happen — maybe it would be best for them to stay far from each other.

He was leaving sometime. And he'd just made it clear he really didn't want her. At least she hadn't thrown herself at him, and it had only been an innocent touch.

"I do have a few things to take care of that Carrie didn't have time for. We can just go over this on Wednesday morning. I'll let you take care of your other projects tomorrow with no interruption."

Stephen nodded and stood up. He slowly moved around the desk without grabbing one of her candies as usual. "I'll see you Wednesday then."

Just before he got out the door completely, Madison remembered her plan to invite him to dinner. "Stephen, wait."

He turned around, his face full of expectation.

"Milo wanted me to invite you to dinner. He didn't get a chance to show you his Legos when you came over while we were sick." Madison knew she was using him as the excuse, but she really did want to have Stephen over for dinner.

Stephen looked at the floor, not meeting her eyes for a moment, and Madison wished she'd never said a thing. He didn't want to come.

"Sure, I'd love to see Milo. How about you text me the details?" He smiled and left the office.

Madison let her head droop.

Chapter Nineteen

Stephen was glad the pitch with the Sharston representatives had gone well. Going to her house for dinner after a bad pitch would have been a little uncomfortable. At least this way, they could talk about work and keep the conversation light if needed. He'd brought another small Lego set, one he thought would be a good addition to Milo's collection, and if he happened to have it already, the pieces would be valuable as additional building materials.

Stephen knocked on the door, happy to see it was Milo who answered again. Madison was fully dressed and standing behind him a few feet. That was unfortunate, since she had looked extra lovely in just the towel. Milo stepped back and motioned for Stephen to come in. Stephen pulled one package from behind his back, almost worried to meet Madison's eyes, but he handed it to Milo. "Just a little gift for the host. You know, it's tradition to bring a gift when invited for the first time."

Madison raised her eyebrows. "This isn't the first time you've been here."

"True," Stephen said. "But it is the first time I didn't invite myself." He pulled his other hand from behind his back and presented the potted orchid. The white blossoms were speckled with a deep pink, and the curved stem was loaded with more than six of them. "And for the hostess."

Madison gasped in surprise. "They're lovely." She reached for them as he cupped the ceramic dish in his other hand to steady it. As she took the pot from him, she met his gaze. "Thank you. They really are beautiful."

He wanted to say they weren't nearly as beautiful as she was, and part of him longed to pluck one of the blossoms and tuck it behind her left ear to show the world she was taken, but she had already turned, taking them farther into the room. Milo had pulled the Lego box out of the gift bag and was over the top in his excitement.

"I wanted this one. Thanks, Stephen." He looked up at Stephen then smiled. "I mean, Dad."

Stephen roughed up Milo's hair. "My pleasure, kiddo. Glad you like it. And maybe you'll let me use it sometimes."

"Yeah, that would be cool." Milo moved over to the little coffee table in the center of the room, the same one where Madison had placed the orchid. He knelt to the side of it and started to open the box, then stopped and looked at Stephen, then his mom. "Can I open this?"

"Sure," Stephen said at the same time Madison said, "Wait till after dinner."

Stephen blanched at the look Madison gave him, but then she glanced at her clock. "I guess it still needs a few minutes to finish cooking. But you'll put it down when dinner's done. Got it?"

Milo nodded. "Got it." He looked at Stephen. "Will you open this, and I'll run grab you one to play with?"

Stephen smiled. "Sure." He took the package from Milo as the kid rushed from the room. Stephen looked up at Madison. She didn't say anything but looked at the package for a minute then turned to the kitchen as Milo returned.

They played for a few minutes, and Stephen grinned at some of the conversations Milo initiated between their little action figures, but it was hard to keep his attention on the toy when he could see Madison alone in the kitchen doing the finishing touches on the meal.

Stephen looked at Milo and knew the kid was so

engaged in his own imagination about building the set that Stephen put his hands on the coffee table to help push himself up. "I'm going to go see if your mom needs any help with dinner or the table, okay?"

Milo nodded and continued playing. Stephen silently approved of the way the kid could keep himself entertained, but he knew how lonely it was to be an only child, even with a ton of cousins. He hoped Milo would be all right. Stephen made his way to the kitchen and caught a glimpse of Madison dancing to the music on her little radio tucked under the cabinet.

Her back was to him, and she wiggled a little to the rhythm, bobbing her head to the beat. She moved with such grace, even in her halfhearted dance attempt. He thought back to the dances he'd attended in King during the Fourth of July celebrations. There weren't a lot of entertainment options there, so the dances during that holiday had been a big deal, and over the years, he'd come to enjoy them. Especially the last one, since he'd danced every dance with Bea. It was hard to reconcile the two women into one. All memories of her from the past were flavored with her small-town roots and her deep love of simplicity and home.

Here, known as Madison, she was a much different person, poised and completely in control, but glimmers of her former self broke through at times, and he longed to have that woman back, the one he'd fallen so hard for, and the one who had opened herself up to him completely, sharing all her hopes and dreams and desires. Yet the woman in front of him was wonderful and amazing in her own right.

A fully grown woman, assured of herself, capable of so much. Tough, when she needed to be, but soft and gentle with her son. She continued to sway to the music as she stirred the pot on the stovetop, and Stephen ignored the little voice that told him to stay back and watch. He slid up next to her, quietly and as gently as possible, so as to not startle her. She stiffened for a moment in surprise, but when he tugged her away from the stove and placed his hand on the small of her back, she didn't protest. He took the hand still holding the spoon in his and did a small spin with her pulled in close to him.

Stephen glanced at the stove to make sure the heat on the pan wasn't too hot then deftly took the spoon out of her hand and slipped it into the pot as he passed the range and swayed with her to the song. Madison giggled as he moved her around the floor in a firm embrace, but not too close.

Oh, how he wanted to be with her, to have the freedom to do this every night, followed by more than just dancing. He spun her around again as the music changed tempo then pulled her close and pressed one hand against her back while holding her hand in his, up against his chest, as he dipped her slowly, meeting her eyes. They sparkled with amusement, but as the music stopped then turned into another song, her expression changed.

It was as if they both realized how close they were, and how right it felt. He pulled her upright ever so slowly, not breaking eye contact with her, afraid to even blink for fear she'd snap out of this moment they were in. He bent down, keeping his eyes locked on hers until he could feel her breath against his skin. He hesitated for just a moment, but she didn't pull back or look away, so he moved a fraction of an inch closer, studying the depth of her eyes.

Her long lashes fluttered closed, and her mouth parted as she raised her chin. Stephen pressed his lips against hers, remembering how ripe they'd always tasted before. But he'd been so young then, so inexperienced, and he didn't want to overwhelm her or make her think he was only in it for the physical. He let them rest softly on hers.

Madison's body seemed to melt against his, and he pulled her closer, glad his hand was still on her back. Her left hand reached up and rested on his bicep as if to hold herself steady. Madison didn't change the kiss, either to break away or make it stronger, but she accepted him, and that sent a thrill through his core.

Stephen gently moved his lips over hers, exploring

the fullness, all the while trying to hold his desire to a reasonable level. With a kid in the next room, he didn't want to be caught in a compromising situation.

As if the thought of Milo had produced the child, Stephen heard him enter the room. "Why ya kissing?" Milo asked.

Madison pulled back as if startled, and Stephen smiled, knowing she had been completely distracted by the kiss.

Milo looked at the two of them then asked, "Are you getting married?"

Madison's mouth dropped open, and her head whipped around to look at Stephen with what he could only describe as panic. She shook her head. "No, Milo. We're not getting married." She turned to the stove and started stirring, ignoring the looks directed at her.

"Then why were you kissing?" Milo asked, fixing his gaze on Stephen.

Stephen took a slow breath, wondering how on earth to answer that question. He looked at Madison's back. "It just felt like the right thing to do at the time." But with that question in the air, did Milo expect them to be together? He wasn't ready for marriage. Not right away. He wanted to make sure they could make things work. Would she give him a chance?

Madison turned to meet his gaze, and Milo, apparently accepting that answer, moved over to the table and pulled out his chair. "Is dinner ready? I'm hungry."

Madison looked at the two men at her table: her little man she'd loved all alone for so long and the grown man she'd loved and cried over so many times. And now they were together, but just not whole. And that kiss. What did it mean? Had he only kissed her because it felt right? Was there any commitment to it? Because she was not willing to go into this just for fun. If she let him into her heart again, she wouldn't let him go. It had hurt too much the first time to lose him.

Right now, Milo's interactions and relationship with Stephen needed to come first. She couldn't do anything to jeopardize their connection. Milo needed to know he was important to both his parents, and if they were too busy with each other, he might fall by the wayside, and she didn't want that.

Chapter Twenty

*F*riday morning, Steven poked his head in Madison's office door but didn't need to knock to get her attention. It was as if she had felt him there and looked up just as he arrived.

"Are you doing anything tonight?"

Madison tilted her head to the side as if she didn't trust his question or the chipper way he'd said it. "No."

"I was wondering what you'd think about doing a movie in. We could do my place or yours." Stephen had hoped she'd say his but wasn't surprised when she answered with a question.

"What movie and is Milo invited?"

"For sure. I need to introduce the kid to *Star Wars*. Can't have a birthday like that and not know about *the force*." Stephen grinned at the mix of amusement on her face.

"I suppose. He's not too young to see that. From

what I remember, it doesn't have too much violence in it, right?" Madison met his eye.

Stephen wondered if he should remind her about all the spaceships blowing up and the off-screen murders happening. "Yeah, totally appropriate for that age. A little bit of action and explosions, but it's all good."

"Okay," Madison agreed. "But I think my place is better. That way I can still get him to bed on time. When should we start?"

Stephen quickly counted back the time in his head. The movie was about two hours, and if he needed to get it done so Milo could go to bed, it would need to start at seven. But he also hoped she'd invite him to stay for a double feature, since he would bring another movie for just the two of them, a romantic comedy he'd overheard her talking about to Kathryn, Mr. Carlson's secretary.

"Is six or six-thirty too early? Or too late?"

"No, that should be fine. It'll give us time to eat dinner and pop some popcorn." She looked up at him. "Do you want to eat with us too?"

Stephen paused for a moment, not sure what to say. If he got there early to eat, would she push him out before the second movie?

"Milo would love to have you come again," Madison added.

Stephen didn't want to disappoint the boy, but also didn't want to overstay his welcome or make her cook for him.

"What if I brought pizza?"

Madison smiled. "Chicago?"

"Absolutely." Stephen pictured her eating it the way they'd done that first night he'd started working here. He hoped she'd make those same little noises as well.

"Sounds great. We'll see you at six then."

Stephen saluted as he left, falling back to the way he'd often said goodbye to her back in King, Montana. She saluted back, and he walked away with a smile on his face.

Madison hurried to her sister's house to pick up Milo. She'd told Karen Thursday morning about the kiss Wednesday night so if Milo mentioned it, Karen wouldn't call her at work. It had been hard to get her to stop asking questions long enough for Madison to leave to make it to the office in time. She'd promised to tell her more about it after work since Karen had needed to rush her kids to soccer practice the night before, but Madison was sure Karen would let her hold off on all the details because of the pizza date with Stephen in a few hours.

When she pulled up to the driveway, both Karen and Milo were standing on the front porch. Madison waved and got out of the car. "Hey kiddo, grab your stuff quick. We're watching a movie tonight with Stephen."

Milo clapped his hands together then turned on his heels and rushed into the house.

Karen's eyes widened, and she gave Madison a long look. She glanced back into the house, not even bothering to close her door, and walked down the steps to meet Madison.

"A movie tonight, huh, and Milo's coming too?"

"It will be at my house. Stephen wants to show Milo *Star Wars* because of his birthday."

"Oh, right. May the fourth be with you." Karen nodded.

"You know about that too?"

Karen giggled. "Jason's a bit of a closet geek."

"I can see that in him, I guess." Madison smiled.

Milo bolted out the door with his backpack and stuff ready to go then joined them at the car and climbed in.

"Hurry, Mom."

Karen leveled her gaze at her sister. "You'd better tell me everything."

"Okay." Madison shrugged. "But if you want to know about the movie, I'm sure you could convince Jason to see it."

"That's not what I'm talking about."

"There won't be anything to tell," Madison insisted. "It's just a movie. And Milo will be there with us."

"Milo was there Wednesday too. That doesn't mean anything."

Madison glanced at her son in the car. "It was a good thing he was there." She took a slow breath and whispered, "I didn't want the kiss to end."

"Good for you. You need a little romance in your life."

Madison shook her head. "No, I need stability and commitment."

Karen placed her hand on Madison's shoulder. "Sometimes they can come from the same person."

"Not so far." Madison frowned.

"Give it a chance this time. Who knows what might happen if you let it."

Madison nodded thoughtfully. That was what she was afraid of.

Stephen knocked on the door, and this time Madison opened it. She smiled at him and welcomed him into the house. He wondered for a second if she was happier to see him or the huge pizza box he held.

"It's still hot. You ready to eat now?"

"Yes!" Milo hollered from the other room.

Madison giggled and shook her head gently then led him into her kitchen. She'd set the table and had a salad made and a pitcher full of some kind of juice. Milo volunteered to pray and was so quick Stephen wondered how long the kid had been waiting to eat. The second he said amen, he opened the box and pulled out a slice.

Milo placed most of it on his plate, only losing a few of the toppings, then proceeded to pick off the things he didn't like. Madison quickly scooped up the topping he'd discarded and added them to her slice. She ate it with a fork this time and didn't moan like she'd done before, but Stephen still watched her eat.

She savored every bite, enjoying the pleasure of the food. It was good to see such a healthy appetite. It made him sure she was the kind to enjoy other things in life.

They chatted happily over dinner, and Stephen helped clean up the table while Madison wrapped the remaining pizza in some tinfoil, separating some into helpings for her to keep and some to send home with

Stephen.

"Can I put the movie in, Mom?" Milo asked.

Madison glanced at Stephen. "Is that okay?"

Stephen nodded.

Madison turned to Milo. "Make sure you open the case carefully. Don't break the disk."

"I won't. I know how to do it now."

Stephen hadn't even considered there might be possible damage. Milo moved into the front room. He opened the DVD case and carefully popped the disk out. He slid it into the player and then did a running jump onto the loveseat, leaving the couch open. Stephen mentally thanked the boy and hoped Milo wouldn't question if Stephen sat close to Madison. If he could convince her to let him.

"Should I push play?" Milo asked.

"In a second," Madison said. She pulled out an air popper and a bag of popcorn kernels.

Even though Stephen had just had two slices of pizza, his mouth watered at the thought of fresh popcorn. She looked at Stephen. "Could you get a stick of butter out of the fridge? Top shelf inside the door."

They worked together to the sound of the popper and had it ready and joined Milo in the front room before he'd asked more than a dozen times about when he could press start.

"Now?" He looked at Madison, and when she

nodded, he pointed the remote at the television and started the show. As the familiar music filled the room and the words scrolled up the screen, Stephen glanced at Milo, who had leaned forward, staring at the words intently. He wasn't sure how much a seven-year-old could read, so Stephen lowered his voice and read the words in his best movie voice-over voice.

"It is a period of civil war. Rebel spaceships, striking from a hidden base…" Stephen continued reading the lines, and Milo grinned at him.

As the movie began, Stephen answered a few questions Milo had about the show until Madison shushed him. "You can ask questions afterward. Just watch and see if the movie answers it for you."

Milo leaned back and pulled the little throw blanket onto his legs and started munching on the bowl of popcorn Madison had given him. She'd placed the other bowl between them, making Stephen just a little disappointed since there wasn't a sneaky way to move over closer to her with it there.

After a few minutes, Milo asked for seconds, so Stephen took the large bowl from the couch and passed it over so he could refill his bowl. When the kid was done, Stephen left it on the end table next to him then glanced at Madison.

"Did you want any more?"

She shook her head. "No, I'm stuffed."

He smiled inwardly. Now that obstacle was out of the way, he just had to decide what kind of move to make. She was leaning against the armrest of the other side, with her bare feet tucked under her legs and a couch pillow on her lap.

The last time they'd watched this movie together, she had been leaning up against him with her legs tucked under her on the other side.

She shifted a few times as if trying to get comfortable, and tilted her head from side to side. He watched her, noticing she kept rolling her shoulders and stretching the back of her neck.

"You feeling okay?" Stephen asked.

"Yeah, just a little bit of a stiff neck. Probably from bending over a laptop so much."

"I could help. I've been told I have magic fingers." Stephen wiggled his fingers at her, smiling when she smiled back. She was the one who had told him his fingers were magic when he used to rub her neck before. He reached for her hand and pulled her toward him. She relented and moved forward then climbed off the couch and put the pillow on the floor at his feet.

He spread his knees open to give her room to sit between them, and she gracefully sat on the floor, her back to him. She reached up and grabbed her hair, twisting it quickly into a bun and tucking the ends underneath to hold it out of the way.

Stephen examined her graceful neck, exposed by her loose, off-the-shoulder shirt. The collar came down in a gentle curve, revealing part of her shoulders, giving him a hint her bra was pink.

He pressed his fingers firmly but gently on the base of her skull. Madison sighed, and Stephen's chest tightened again. She had no idea what those sounds did to him, but he wanted to hear more of them, so he began working his magic, still very aware there was a child on the love seat next to them.

Chapter Twenty-one

*M*adison sighed. Stephen really did have magic fingers. The knots that had plagued her for days were finally loosening, and she thought she might actually get rid of the strain of the last few days. It was nice that the man who had put those knots there in the first place was taking them away.

He'd been working on the achy muscles for at least ten minutes and didn't show any signs of stopping. She wasn't going to tell him to quit either. He was better than a paid masseuse. Stephen moved from the base of her skull and the tight muscles around her spine to the shoulders, gently kneading them.

He spent some time on one side then moved to the other, never pushing harder than necessary, but applying the perfect amount of pressure. As he worked another knot, Madison sighed again, the pleasure too much to hold back. She glanced at Milo, who was engrossed in the film, and then glanced back toward Stephen but couldn't see much more than his knees and forearms.

She turned her head straight and just let him continue. With a quiet whisper, he instructed her to move forward a little, pressing his palms against her back until she was leaning forward. He worked her long back muscles, taking slow purposeful strokes down the muscles on each side of her spine.

He worked those for a few minutes then took one hand and placed it on her shoulder, guiding her back into more of an upright position. As he pressed on one spot, Madison grunted in discomfort at the stubborn knot. He kneaded that for a moment, but because of where it was, Madison kept leaning forward with the pressure from his hands.

Stephen slid further to the edge of the couch and leaned forward, placing his left arm around her shoulder and crossing it over just under her collarbone, then wrapped his warm hand around her right bicep to hold her steady. Her body stiffened in surprise at the contact. His closeness should have worried her, but it felt so good she didn't want him to stop.

She relaxed, allowing him to hold her steady as he worked the offending muscle into submission. He didn't overwork any one area, but moved from place to place then returned to the areas of tight muscles until she didn't feel the former stiffness. As he worked his way lower down her back, she could tell he was bending over to try to reach it.

"You don't have to keep going," Madison said, though she wished with all her heart he would never stop.

"Can't give you a half massage," Stephen whispered. "Here, sit up." He pointed to the couch and shifted his body to the side a little.

She did as he instructed and sat on the couch, feeling the warmth of his large hands as he placed them on the curve of her hips to guide her where to sit.

He pressed his thumbs on both sides of the spine, and she moaned again. Stephen's fingers tightened on her hips for a moment. His thumbs eased up, then he began again, and Madison let herself just relax until she felt limp. As he finished working her lower back, he pulled her close to him until her shoulder was tucked under his as his arm wrapped around her, allowing her to snuggle against him.

They fit together so perfectly, and she felt absolutely amazing. The logical part of her mind told her to thank him and move to her side of the couch, but the other side, the traitorous one who only knew how lonely she was, didn't want to move.

What would it hurt to just stay here throughout the rest of the movie? Stephen didn't put his hands anywhere they shouldn't be. The hand that held her close was softly resting on her forearm. She closed her eyes and took a slow cleansing breath.

She could easily stay here the entire night.

Stephen stared at the top of Madison's head as she snuggled into him. He couldn't believe it worked as smoothly as it had. The suggestion to work out the tension in her muscles had been completely innocent to begin with, but once he felt her soft skin beneath his fingers, he hadn't been able to help himself and had continued on. Each time he'd moved from one muscle group to the next, he'd hoped she wouldn't put an end to it, and now that she was in his arms, he couldn't be more pleased with himself.

He glanced at Milo, who didn't seem to even notice the two of them on the couch. Stephen had peeked at the kid a few times, making sure his son was okay with him touching his mom, and hoping he wouldn't say anything that might wake Madison out of the trance he'd worked so hard to put her under.

And though he hadn't watched more than a few minutes of the movie tonight, he couldn't help thinking *Star Wars* was the best movie ever. He turned his attention back to Madison, straining his head a little to see if he could see her face, but she had her forehead pointed down a little.

He listened close, feeling her breathing motions as her chest rose and fell. He wasn't positive, but he thought she was asleep.

He leaned his head back against the couch and settled in to watch the rest of the movie, happier than he had been in months.

He still couldn't believe his luck that he had been hired at the same company where Madison worked. Too bad he would only be there for another month on his contract. She was too good at what she did to make his services necessary longer than that.

Chapter Twenty-two

*M*adison shifted in her sleep against Stephen, and he held still, not wanting to jostle her. The movie had ended, and Milo had asked if they could watch another movie. Stephen agreed, hoping Madison wouldn't be upset that he was still here, but she was sleeping so soundly he didn't want to wake her.

She must have overworked herself to be this completely gone. It was past eleven, and Milo's choice of movie was almost over, and the kid had fallen asleep on the loveseat, one leg hanging half off and his mouth open. Stephen smiled then turned his face to look at Madison.

His arm had gotten numb a few times, and he had shifted slightly to ease the pressure of her head against him, but it felt so good to hold her he hadn't minded the tingling sensations developing in his fingers.

What he wanted to do was stretch out onto the

couch and snuggle her body next to him, but with the movie wrapping up, he knew he should excuse himself and let them head to bed. If he hadn't been trapped by Madison's body, he would have carried Milo to his room, and maybe he could still do that after he woke her.

He brought his free hand up and stroked her hair then softly rubbed her shoulder. That didn't wake her, so he squeezed her arm and whispered, "Madison."

She stirred a little, then, as if coming to her full senses, sat up straight and stared at him.

"Oh, Stephen." She rubbed her face. "I'm sorry. I didn't mean to fall asleep. How rude of me."

"No worries. I didn't mind."

Madison looked at the TV. "This isn't *Star Wars*. How long was I out?" She looked around the dark room as if searching for a clock. "Did you start a different movie?" She looked over at Milo sleeping on the couch then at Stephen.

He couldn't tell in the dark what her eyes held in them. He hoped she wasn't bothered. It was a weekend, and she didn't have to get up early for work.

"Milo wanted to watch this one. I thought it would be okay."

Madison nodded. "He loves that movie." She relaxed a little, leaning into the couch but not touching Stephen anymore.

He wanted to take her hand but instead leaned against the back of the couch and turned enough that he was closer to her and face to face.

She tilted her head to the side, smiled sweetly, and whispered, "I'm just glad I didn't have to watch it."

Stephen chuckled. "It wasn't that bad."

"Yeah, the first time you see it. But after a couple dozen times, it gets a little annoying."

"Didn't you have a favorite movie growing up?" Stephen asked.

"Yeah, probably." She looked up at the ceiling. "I can't think of what it was though."

They talked for a few minutes about the movies and shows they watched as kids and giggled a few times as they quoted lines. Madison did a perfect imitation of an actress, making Stephen laugh loud enough to startle Milo. He rolled off the couch and hit the floor with a thud, not catching himself at all.

He was still so deep into sleep he only fussed for a moment then whimpered as he struggled to get comfortable on the floor. Madison had jumped off the couch and rushed over to him then shook her head in amusement that he was still asleep.

"Would you like me to carry him to his bed?" Stephen asked.

"He's kinda heavy."

Stephen flexed his arm then did a few bodybuilder

poses, and Madison giggled. "Okay, Mr. Universe, you can take him."

He bent down and lifted the boy then followed Madison to his room and placed him on the bed after she'd pulled the covers down. Something about the moment felt right, as if he should have done this thousands of times over the last seven years. A wave of sadness followed by a flash of anger at being denied this privilege struck him, and he focused his gaze on Milo instead of looking at Madison.

She should have told him. She should have trusted him and not listened to the lies her parents had told her about him. He turned to her to ask why, but she wiped her eyes and looked up at him.

"Thank you for being so good with him."

He nodded and followed her out of the room, closing the door as he went. She continued into the front room, and he joined her as she gathered the throw pillows and blankets. He took the popcorn bowl, drink cups, and Milo's bowl into the kitchen then returned to see her standing in front of the television.

"I didn't know you brought this one." She held up the romantic comedy.

"Yeah, I thought we could watch it after *Star Wars* if it wasn't too late."

"Maybe another time." She held it out to him, but he didn't take it.

"I don't have to get up early. And you've had a nap…"

Madison smiled. "I have wanted to see this."

"So stick it in."

She hesitated for a moment, looking down the hallway toward Milo's room then at the clock and down at the disk in her hand. "Okay."

She bent down to put the movie in, and Stephen returned to his corner of the couch. He didn't hug the armrest, but tried not to take up too much space so she would chose the loveseat Milo no longer occupied or even suck herself into the other corner.

When she sat down, she was only a few inches away, and he leaned back against the couch, purposely shifting his shoulders to lean toward her. She leaned back as well, and her head tilted toward his. She glanced at him, and he met her eyes. "You aren't going to fall asleep, are you?"

He smiled. "No promises. I didn't have a nap today, so it all depends on how much this movie keeps my attention." As the opening scenes began, he dramatically yawned, tilted his head further to the side until it leaned against her shoulder, and started snoring theatrically.

"Shut up." She giggled. "I've heard it's a good one."

He stopped snoring but left his head resting on

her shoulder. She didn't move away and let her head rest against his. Stephen smiled. He'd sit through any movie she wanted as long as he could be by her. And if he were lucky, he might be able to sneak in a kiss or two.

Madison struggled to stay focused on the movie. With Stephen in her home so late at night and them practically alone, she felt strange and a little naughty. Her son, their son, was sleeping sounding in the room down the hall, but she was basically alone with this man who sent shivers of longing down every inch of her body at the slightest thing. He looked at her in a way that made her melt. His touch was comforting, yet stimulating, and sent her emotions into a whirlwind of desire.

And now that she was snuggled on the couch next to him, she just wanted to make out with him like they'd done as teens. That kiss on Wednesday had reopened her eyes to how much she had missed over the years. She didn't regret not dating. It had just been easier not to, and she hadn't wanted to put Milo through the turmoil of her break-ups. Besides, not many guys were that interested in getting involved with a single mother. But the guilt at having deprived Stephen of the chance to be with his son dug at her.

She still didn't know how much she wanted to let him into her life. She knew the attraction was there. They could be physically happy and satisfied — she had no doubt. But would he be good for them in the long run? She knew he'd changed since she'd last seen him. But how much?

And would he be the kind to step into an instant family? Because she didn't want it to just be casual. If she allowed him in, she wanted him for good. Milo needed stability. She needed stability. That's why she'd worked so hard to buy this little house instead of just finding a rental apartment.

She turned her attention back to the movie, then a few minutes later, Stephen shifted a little, taking his head off her shoulder for a moment and angling his body more solidly on the couch. He rested his head again on her shoulder and placed his hand on her leg, just above the knee.

She looked at it for a moment, knowing exactly what he was doing. In a few minutes, he would bring his hand a little higher then let it rest and work his way up a little until he could place his hand on the hip furthest away from him and pull her into a side embrace. She debated for a moment on whether to take his hand in hers and hold it still so he couldn't continue on his planned path or to let it run its course and enjoy the teasing.

As he slid his hand up a bit, she smiled inside and let the butterflies have their way. When he moved it to halfway between her hip and knee, she knew the butterflies would turn into dragonflies, driving her crazy. Deciding to throw caution off the back of the couch, she turned to him. "I know that move," she whispered, leaning closer to him.

Stephen lifted his head in apparent surprise, and she smiled at the confused expression. "Move?" Stephen said. "What move?"

Madison placed her hand on his leg, just above the knee, feeling the strong muscles beneath the fabric of his pants. She then moved it a little higher and met his eyes. He studied her, not speaking, but swallowed when she moved the hand a little higher. "Then, in a couple minutes, you'd have done this." She reached across him and placed her hand on his waist. She leaned her head against his chest until she could feel the pounding of his heart.

"Why, Ms. Perry," Stephen said after a moment, "that's quite the move you've got down."

She lifted her head, still keeping her hand on him, but it slid across his belly as she sat up enough to see his face. He trapped her fingers under his, keeping her from moving further away, and she froze, not sure what to do.

She knew what she wanted to do. Her body remembered other things, though she hadn't done anything like that for years. This time, she wanted to do it right. To be in a lasting committed relationship. And for Milo's sake, as well as her own, she would wait until she was married.

As she stared into Stephen's dark eyes, barely visible in the dim room with just the light from the television, she caved a little. What would it hurt to kiss him again? She leaned forward and pressed a soft kiss against his cheek then moved closer to tease the corner of his mouth lightly with her tongue. He let go of her hand and turned more toward her, and she kissed his lips, enjoying the sensations it brought.

After a few minutes, she pulled back. Stephen searched her eyes then took a slow breath. "I think that move was my favorite so far."

Madison smiled and pressed closer again, feeling his arms wrap around her as he pulled her back against him on the couch. She stretched out next to him for a moment, then he shifted her again to a more comfortable position and deepened the kiss. She joined him in it and kissed him back just as intently, her hands exploring his arms while his caressed her back, eventually finding their way under her shirt.

He pulled back a little, and she paused, feeling

surprised.

He searched deep into her eyes and whispered, "Let me stay?"

Her body screamed yes, practically begged her to answer him, but as memories of what had happened before promised her happiness, she knew it was fleeting. And it was too soon to head down this path again. She had to keep her head straight. Think with more than just emotions this time.

His eyes had never left hers, and she knew the moment he saw the decision in her eyes.

"I'm sorry. I'm not ready for that," Madison whispered.

Stephen nodded and released his hold on her back.

She pushed herself away from him slowly, wishing for a moment she'd given him a different answer, but she knew this was the right one. She moved over to her side of the couch, and Stephen sighed.

"Then I'd better leave now. You're too much temptation for me to stay longer."

Madison nodded. "I'm sorry."

"Me too." Stephen rubbed his hands across his face then into his hair.

He stood without looking at her, and Madison felt rejected even though she'd been the one who'd told him to stop. As he grabbed his shoes he'd kicked off during the first film, she wiped a tear from her eye then stood up to get the movie out.

When she pressed stop, he spoke again. "You can keep it for the night. Go ahead and finish it. I'll get it later." He walked over to her and bent down to kiss the top of her head. "Thanks for dinner and a movie."

He turned and left, and as he closed the door, she sat back on the couch and stared at the black television screen. Had she done the right thing?

Stephen rested his head against the steering wheel for a moment before starting the car. He was moving too fast and, given how things had progressed before, she probably thought the only thing he wanted was sex. He should never have asked to stay. He should have eased up on the kissing and told her they should take things slow. Let her know he could be a gentleman and in control of himself.

Instead, he'd practically seduced her in her living room and begged to take her to bed. She was just too desirable to keep his mind together. He would need to back off and let this relationship progress at the right speed. Not try to go too fast just because they'd been involved before. And while they worked together, he couldn't go far anyway. Mr. Carlson wouldn't appreciate him making this professional relationship too personal.

Once his contract was over, he'd be free to pursue her the right way. He'd have to talk to Mr. Carlson about how much longer he was needed. Until then, he'd keep things strictly business. He started the car and drove away.

Chapter Twenty-three

*M*adison had sent a text to Stephen the next morning, asking if he was interested in meeting for lunch at the park with her and Milo, but he'd responded that he wasn't able to make it and asked for a raincheck.

Milo acted slightly disappointed but occupied himself with playing in his room.

Madison spent the rest of the morning worried that Stephen was mad at her for turning him down last night. The more she thought about that, the more annoyed she became. She had the right to make that choice. And if he couldn't accept that, it just proved she was right to refuse him. He needed to act like an adult. And if he was going to pout, she'd deal with it the same way she handled Milo. Hold firm and wait out his tantrum.

On Monday morning as Madison pulled into her

parking spot, she saw Stephen walking toward the building. She waved at him, and he nodded then entered the building without waiting for her. She grabbed her bag and worked her way to her office, still puzzling over his behavior. If he was still upset about having been turned down, then he was definitely not the type of mature man she needed.

They would be meeting this morning to go over the potential client list again to see which ones to follow up with, and see if there were any new angles they could use to capture the attention of the others. It would be an interesting morning.

Madison filled the candy dish out of habit and contemplated adding some extra Butterfingers. She decided against it and just left it how it was and sat down at her desk. She bent her head down toward her laptop, and memories of the wonderful massage from Friday night made her adjust her head to avoid straining her neck. She didn't think he'd be giving her another massage any time soon.

After working for an hour, she wondered where Stephen was. He should have come in to start the collaboration. She debated calling his office then shook her head and focused on getting her accounts up to date. She glanced up now and then as people passed her door, expecting to see him any moment, but time kept passing without any sign of him.

Madison fumed in annoyance. This was very unprofessional of him. If he couldn't keep his personal life from affecting his business behavior, she didn't want to even see the guy again. From the corner of her eye, she saw Stephen's large frame walking toward her office. *Finally he shows up.* Before he reached her door, someone called his name. He raised his eyes to look at Carrie who'd joined him.

Madison couldn't hear them, but they were being very friendly, and Carrie was obviously working all the moves she could on him.

Madison fought down the flash of jealousy that rose like bile from the pit of her stomach. She watched as Carrie placed her hand on his chest and let her fingers trail down his front a couple inches before she turned playfully away and added a bit of sway to her walk that wasn't always there.

Stephen watched her go, an unreadable expression on his face. Madison looked down at her own shorter legs and wider hips and deflated. She could never compete against that, and she knew it. Anger washed over her, and she kept her eyes down, not daring to look at Stephen until she could get herself under control. She hoped he would just walk away and not come into her office, but no sooner had that thought crossed her mind than he knocked on her door.

Madison lifted her head slowly, trying to force her

face into her professional smile. She met his eyes, daring him to give a good-enough excuse for his behavior.

"Do you have time now to go over the client lists?" Stephen asked.

Madison's mouth opened then she closed it, knowing she shouldn't say what she wanted to about his lateness. She nodded curtly. "I do have time, but not long. I have some things to take care of on the Sharston account this afternoon."

Stephen nodded. "I left my laptop in my office. Do I need it, or do you have the information there?"

"I have it all," Madison said. "But I'm not going to transcribe your chicken scratch again, so no paper."

Stephen's eyes widened just a fraction as if he didn't understand where that had come from. Madison didn't even know why she'd brought it up. It had just jumped out of her mouth as a lame attempt to hurt him. Madison looked down at the laptop as an excuse to not look at him.

She wasn't being very professional, and it shamed her. She needed to do better, and the best way to be professional was to not get involved emotionally. Keep it all on the surface. And to do that, she needed to shut Stephen out of her thoughts completely and instead focus on working with Mr. Kohalohini.

Besides, it was obvious he didn't want to be

involved with her. Not after she'd told him no. So she'd give him his wish. "We have a couple new potential clients here. One is a promising new startup company working out of their home office. The other is a small business that has opened two new locations." Madison went over the list, explaining the options they had and what they could do to get them to sign like the others they'd discussed.

Stephen nodded, moved around the desk, and looked at the screen. Madison turned it toward him to keep him from coming too close. That was the last thing she needed right now. Fighting her heart was harder to do when his presence was so *in your face*. Keeping him at a safe distance would allow her to keep her brain in charge and avoid any of the messes that would come from being involved with a co-worker.

Stephen felt the coldness just oozing off Madison. Her body language shouted at him to keep his distance, and, after having pushed his luck a little too much on Friday night, he decided to listen to his gut. He would ease up some, and instead of sliding close to her like he wanted, he kept his chair a couple feet away from hers and studied the computer screen when she turned it to him.

She discussed the client list with the efficiency of a long-time employee, and he wondered again why she wasn't doing this job more than the accounts she had been finishing up when he'd come onboard. Mr. Carlson really didn't need to pay Stephen's fee when he had this untapped goldmine working for him already.

As soon as she was done, she turned the computer back toward her, and Stephen debated on what to do. He wanted to talk to her, bring up the movie and the kiss, but she angled her body away from him. He reached for a mini candy bar to give him something to do while he tried to figure out what to say.

"If you'll excuse me, I have some calls to make." Madison didn't even look at him but kept busy on her computer.

Stephen stood slowly and returned the chair to its original location. He kept his hands on the back of the chair, trying to keep from looking nervous. "Are we still on for meeting at the park with Milo?" It was always easier to be with her around the kid.

Madison finally looked up at him, but her eyes were less than warm. "Tonight isn't a great night. He was invited to his cousin Max's soccer game, and he'd really like to go."

"Does Milo play?" Stephen asked.

Madison shook her head.

"Why not?" Stephen asked, curious about whether the kid was interested in any sports.

"I couldn't afford the fees involved." Madison stared at him as if she were daring him to say anything more about it.

He hesitated, wondering if she'd allow him to help pay for something like that.

Instead of asking what he wanted, he tried a different tactic. "Does he go to his cousin's games often?"

Madison watched him for a moment then nodded. "Sometimes. Depends on the time of day, and if he's already with Karen."

"What time's the game?" Stephen asked. "Can I come?"

Madison opened her mouth then closed it. He was almost certain she was going to tell him no, but then she put on a smile he knew wasn't genuine. "I don't think watching a bunch of seven-year-olds play soccer would be all that interesting to you. Why don't you wait until tomorrow, and you can see him."

Stephen nodded. It was better than nothing. "We could go to the park again. Would you like me to pick you up?"

Madison stared at him for a moment. "I'm sure Milo would love the park. In fact, I guess it's time for you two to do something on your own, if you're ready to try it solo."

Stephen pulled one hand off the back of the chair and stuck it in his pocket. She was actually trusting him enough to let her son go with him alone? That was a huge step, and though he would really love to have her there with them, he would take this chance and run with it. Show her he could be a good dad.

"Yeah, that sounds good. Besides, you probably have things you'd like to do on your own." He took a step back. "I'll check with you tomorrow about the specifics. Thanks, Madison."

She nodded then turned her attention back to her computer, shutting him out again. It might take a while to warm her back up to him, but he would do it. He'd go slowly, stay at the pace she needed until she finally accepted him into her life for good. After having held her in his arms the other night, he knew he wanted her for the rest of his life. And Milo needed his father. He was sure of it.

As he turned around and walked out of her office, he heard his name called. "Stephen, wait up a moment," Carrie said as she approached him. "Mr. Carlson would like to see you in his office."

Stephen looked past her toward his boss's office. "Thanks."

"No problem." She took a step closer and looked at his face. She hesitated a second then reached up and brushed the corner of his mouth with her thumb. "You have some chocolate on your face."

He chuckled nervously and wiped his mouth. "Thanks. Didn't realize I was that sloppy when I ate."

"Yeah, it's always a good idea to look your best when you see the boss." She reached up and fixed his tie. "This needs just a little straightening." She brushed off his shoulders and adjusted his suit coat. "There. Perfect." Her hands lingered on his arm a moment.

Stephen took her hand and gently removed it from his arm. He took a step back, hoping she'd get the hint he wasn't available.

"Good luck," Carrie said, smiling.

"Thanks." Stephen nodded, but didn't return the smile before heading to Mr. Carlson's office.

Madison watched Carrie throw herself at Stephen again, and he seemed to love every second of her attentions. She wanted to hate Carrie, but what good would that do? And it would only make things more awkward here at work.

Besides, Stephen really didn't belong to her. And if he wanted to chase other women, she couldn't stop him. No, it just proved how unreliable Stephen was, and that she was better off keeping him out of her heart even though he was back in her life because of her son.

Chapter Twenty-four

Stephen smiled at the secretary as he approached Mr. Carlson's office. "Aloha, Kathryn."

Kathryn grinned wide. "Stephen, good to see you. Mr. Carlson said to go right in."

Stephen nodded, relieved it wasn't a formal affair where he would have to wait outside the office. The Carlson Ad Agency had just the right mix of professional and family atmosphere to go far in this business. He knocked twice then opened the door partway to double-check that it was a good time. Mr. Carlson waved him in, and Stephen closed the door behind him.

"Thanks for coming in. Have a seat. How are we coming along?" Mr. Carlson put his pen down and focused his attention on Stephen.

Stephen sat down and leaned back in the chair.

"Really well. Madison is doing amazing at it. In fact, I think she'd be much better utilized by having her there full time, instead of controlling the accounts." If he could talk her up to the boss and get her the raise and promotion she deserved, that ought to help him win some points with her.

Mr. Carlson nodded. "I've wondered on that myself. She seems to be a natural at it. When Robert asked her for help at the beginning, she was hesitant, but she always steps in to help where needed. He mentioned many times that she seems to know exactly what will work for a particular client."

Stephen smiled. "I don't mean to talk myself out of a job, but she probably could have done this without me."

Mr. Carlson's face turned serious. "Really?"

Stephen nodded. "Most everything I've suggested she already knew about or was working on something similar. She mentioned she was hesitant to branch out too much into the social media aspects because she indicated you and Robert preferred your usual formats, and it was still technically Robert's arena. However, if you give her a little bit of free reign, I think you'll be pleased with what she comes up with. I've worked with her on a lot of the upcoming proposals, but most of the ideas have come from her. I've just steered her in the right direction."

Mr. Carlson smiled. "Wonderful. So in your opinion, we're on the right track?"

Stephen nodded. "Yes, and if you get someone to cover the accounts Madison is still working on in her spare time, you'll find she'll have more clients signed in no time."

"And this has nothing to do with the fact you two have a history?" Mr. Carlson eyed Stephen. "You aren't trying to sway me because of how you feel about her or your son?"

Stephen smiled. Of course the boss would put things together. "I do admire her and can't deny there are feelings of a personal nature, but there is nothing like that in this recommendation. She really is a fantastic employee. And since I don't plan to stay here with Carlson long-term, and Robert isn't in a position to return right away, putting Madison over the new client acquisitions is really your best option."

Mr. Carlson looked at his office door as if considering things. Stephen tucked his hands behind his back. "Carrie was really efficient with the accounts while Madison was out sick last week."

Mr. Carlson nodded. "True. I'll look into where I can shift things." He looked up at Stephen. "Now, about the rest of your contract?"

Stephen smiled. "It's up to you. I could leave now and give you a discount or stay on for the next month to help Madison transition into this spot. But I did get an offer with another company who wants me as soon as possible."

Mr. Carlson stood and offered his hand to Stephen. "If she's as good as you say she is, I'm all for discounts. I'd like you to stay for the rest of this week so we can make sure everything is in order."

"Done." Stephen took Mr. Carlson's hand and sealed the deal.

One more week working closely with Madison would help him figure out where to go next. If she still needed space, he could take the offer from the company in Oregon and go there in person. That job wouldn't be as intensive as what Carlson Ad Agency had needed, but he would have to go up for a few days at least. Maybe if he gave her the space she needed for a while, he could return when things eased up and she was ready to see him again.

Chapter Twenty-five

Stephen knocked on Madison's front door Tuesday night, hoping she would answer. She had still refused his offer to come with them when he'd talked to her at the office. And she had spent the day catching up on the accounts and had begged off any collaboration meetings with him. It didn't seem like Mr. Carlson had let her know yet about shifting her into the other department, but he had told her he wanted the accounts in order as soon as possible. At least she would be passing that job on to Carrie soon. He hoped to give one last invite before he and Milo headed to the park.

Instead, his smiling son greeted him at the door then turned around and hollered into the house. "Mom, Dad is here."

"Okay, have fun, buddy."

"See ya!" He stepped out of the house and pulled

the door shut before Stephen had a chance to bring up the subject of inviting Madison. "I'm so excited. Where are we going? Does it have to be the same park Mom always takes me to? I know one that has dinosaurs, but she never wants to go there. I asked Aunt Karen to write down the address, so I have it." Milo shoved his hand into his front pocket and pulled out a crumpled note. "Mom always says it's too far away and that we don't have much time to go since she has to get home to make dinner, but since she's not coming, maybe we could go?" Milo stopped talking and held his breath.

Stephen's smile widened. "Sure, kiddo. I think I can find this address." He typed the numbers into his phone for the map directions. "How do you know about this park?"

"It was by the field where Max played a game. When I got bored, I took Carley over to it, and we had lots of fun. I really wanted to go again."

"Did you not watch the soccer game?" Stephen asked.

Milo shrugged. "A little, but it's always the same thing, so Carley and I were bored."

"Max and Carley are your cousins, right?"

"Yup. Max is eight, and Carley is six."

"Do you ever want to play soccer?" Stephen asked. He hoped he wouldn't get in trouble with Madison, but he wanted to know if he could help get the kid involved if he wanted to play

"Not really. Max likes it, but I'd rather just play something else. And he has lots of practices so he can't do other things."

Stephen nodded. "That's cool. But if you ever want to start playing soccer, let me know. We'll see what we can do about getting you on a team."

Milo shrugged. "Okay." He walked over to the car and waited while Stephen pushed the unlock button. He peeked into the back seat. "There isn't a booster in here."

"I think you're big enough to not need one."

Milo grinned up at him. "Really?" He glanced back at the house. "Mom says I'm still supposed to be in one."

"I think we'll be fine." Stephen smiled when Milo jumped into the car and situated himself then pulled his seat belt across his lap and adjusted the strap. Stephen slid into his seat and started the car, listening to the happy chatter of the kid in the back and the driving instructions on his navigator.

The time alone with Milo turned out to be just what he'd needed. It was nice to ask him questions about his childhood without his mother there to think he was judging her for raising him alone. Milo was a very well-adjusted child, and it was obvious his mother loved him and took good care of him. He also had a strong relationship with his aunt and uncle, for which Stephen was grateful.

When Stephen asked about his grandparents, Milo shrugged. "We don't go visit very often. Mom doesn't have a lot of vacation time. They come see us sometimes. They're fun, I guess."

"That's good," Stephen said. "Do you do anything fun when they come?"

"Yeah, Grandpa likes to take us to the zoo. He really likes the animals there."

"Do you like the zoo?" Stephen asked. "Should we plan a trip?"

"Yeah, I guess. I like seeing the tigers the most. They're really cool. They aren't as lazy as the lions are. And the monkeys are kinda cool too. But there's this one monkey that has a purple bum…" Milo continued explaining all about the animals he liked to see at the zoo until they reached the park.

"Is this the right one?" Stephen asked as he pulled into the parking spot.

"Yup, this is it." Milo unbuckled himself and opened the door. "Hey, your door works."

"Of course it works."

"Mom's door doesn't open from the inside. I have to wait for her to open it."

Stephen nodded. She must have the child-lock switch on in the back seat. But Milo was seven, so

Stephen doubted he had to worry about that with him. Maybe the kid needed a few chances to explore the world without being so structured. At least Madison had let him bring Milo alone. Even if it was probably because she didn't want to see him right then.

He needed to figure out how to break her hard shell again. Maybe he could get some information out of Milo. But how observant was a kid his age?

Madison watched from her window as Milo and Stephen got in the car. She saw Milo hesitate at the back door of the car and realized Stephen didn't have a booster seat. He was technically supposed to be in one, but she'd let it slide. And he was old enough he could go on an outing with his father unsupervised, but the thought of sending him away like this ate at her. He was her baby that wasn't a baby anymore, and it was hard to admit he needed someone besides her.

She'd made the mistake of telling Milo Stephen wanted an outing, just the two of them, in a weak moment when she didn't want to go because she couldn't bear to be with Stephen.

He was too good-looking, and it was hard to keep her mind on the right things when all she could think about was the way they'd been last week. She had almost fallen for him again, and it had been so easy. She wanted it so much, but he wasn't interested in her more than just the physical. And his ego was too fragile to handle the rejection.

But at least he was still trying to be a part of Milo's life. She couldn't fault him for that. Milo needed him, even if she didn't. If Stephen was going to be here for a while, she needed to get over her anger at him and find a way to work with him.

Chapter Twenty-six

*S*tephen stood at her office door Thursday morning, watching as she studied her computer screen again, ignoring him even though he was sure she'd seen him approach. He knew she didn't want to see him, but he needed to make sure things were right between him before he left the company for good tomorrow. When Mr. Carlson had called her into his office yesterday, Stephen hadn't been there, so he didn't know how she'd taken the news of his leaving or of her promotion. But this didn't bode well.

He knocked on the door, and she brought her head up slowly. The look in her eyes made him leery. He took a stabilizing breath and stepped into the room. "How's it going?"

She narrowed her eyes at him. "I'm swamped. Thanks to you."

"You're welcome." He grinned, trying to make

light of the situation. "We've brought in a bunch of new clients to Carlson. You should be proud of yourself."

Madison's anger deflated just a touch, but he knew he would have to tread carefully. She didn't speak again but looked back at the computer.

"You can do this job with your eyes closed, Madison. Don't fret, just do what you've been doing, and you'll be fine."

"I didn't want this job," Madison said. "I was happy where I was."

Stephen didn't believe that. At least not much. He knew she'd bristled at the thought he had been training her on something she was doing well at anyway.

"And now I've got to get this done to pass it over to Carrie and then take care of all this new stuff on my own."

She pressed her lips together, and Stephen wondered what kind of comment she was biting back. He'd gotten familiar enough with her to know she stopped herself from saying things she shouldn't. It was a good quality, but it was frustrating as well.

"Then I'll let you get to it. But before I go, I wondered if you'd let me take you to dinner. Just the two of us."

Madison looked up once more briefly then shook her head and looked back at the computer. "I don't think that's a good idea. I'll be working through the weekend getting this ready so I can transition into the new position." She paused for a moment then glanced at him. "Maybe next week sometime." The way she said it sounded like she was trying to mollify him.

Stephen frowned. "I'll be gone on Monday. Heading to Oregon for a new job."

Madison's body froze for a second, then she nodded curtly. "Got it."

"I'll be back on the weekends," Stephen said. "I'd like to keep seeing Milo as often as possible, but I'm not sure how long this job will be, or where I'll go next." He could work from home on some accounts, but the ones he went to in person always brought in a higher fee.

Madison nodded. "Of course. He'd be disappointed if you left for long, but he's a tough kid."

Stephen wished she would miss him as well, but he knew it was probably too much to ask. At least with Milo, he'd be able to work on her a little bit at a time.

"Great. I'll call him during the week too."

Madison sighed. "Look, I appreciate you being there for Milo, but I really need to get this done." She looked at the door, her expression clear that she didn't want to see him anymore.

"Right. Good luck, Madison."

She didn't respond, and he left feeling like he'd

just messed up but afraid to make things worse by going back while she was so angry. He didn't know what to do, so he headed to his office to finish packing his things.

As Stephen left her office, Madison closed her heart for good. She should have known he would have left again. At least this time, he would still be there for Milo. But it was obvious he didn't want to be a part of her life except through him. And he'd left her with so much on her plate, she didn't have time to cry for him. Besides, she'd cried all the tears she ever wanted to on the man. He didn't deserve any more of them.

Later that night, Madison headed toward her front door as Milo shouted that he would answer it. She always checked to make sure who it was, even though Milo knew to check the peephole before answering.

"It's Dad," Milo said, and Madison froze in the hallway. He hadn't told her he was coming, and it was too late to take Milo anywhere.

"Hi, Milo," Stephen said when the door opened to reveal him. He stood there filling her doorway but didn't enter. He caught her eye then looked back at Milo. "I needed to come talk to you in person before I left. I have to leave earlier than planned and wanted to see if we could reschedule our trip to the zoo for next week."

Milo's shoulders sagged, and it hurt Madison's heart to see his disappointment. So this is how it would go.

"Yeah, I guess," Milo said.

As Stephen pulled out a box from against the side of the door, Milo straightened, and Madison's eyes narrowed.

"I know it's not the same as the zoo, but maybe this Lego zoo set would hold you over for a bit." Stephen smiled wide at Milo's enthusiastic response.

"Awesome. Thanks, Dad."

Stephen didn't look at her, and it was a good thing, because Madison wasn't sure if she could maintain her cool in front of Milo. The idiot man knew she didn't want him bribing her son, but apparently it didn't matter what she said or thought. He would do whatever he wanted, no thought of how anyone else felt.

"I have to run soon, got to catch my flight. I'll talk to you later, kiddo. Okay?" Stephen said, bending down to Milo's level. He opened his arms for a hug, and Milo hugged him quickly then picked up the Lego box again. "Go take that to your room so I can talk to your mom a second."

Milo nodded and rushed past Madison, slowing down long enough to lift the box and say, "Look, Mom. This is so cool."

Madison nodded but didn't need to respond since the boy was off again, running toward his room. She looked up to see Stephen watching her.

"I'm sorry to rush off like this, but I've already talked to Mr. Carlson, and he's good with it. This offer is too good to pass up. I'll be back for a follow-up consultation in a few weeks. I'm not worried about you. You've got these pitches down."

Madison watched him, waiting for something personal, an apology to her for leaving without closure to their relationship, but it was all about work and Milo. At least she knew where she stood with him. She didn't speak, and he didn't either. He shifted his weight onto another foot, then an alarm beeped, and he looked down at his watch.

"I've got to go. I'll keep in touch."

Madison nodded numbly. She didn't want to expect anything from him. The less emotion she put into their strange relationship, the better she'd be.

Chapter Twenty-seven

Madison didn't have much time to miss Stephen that next week. They'd scheduled two pitches that week, and she was left to do them all on her own, with Mr. Carlson watching as if waiting to see her fail. Carrie had called in sick for the first two days of the week, and Madison had taken care of the accounts and the pitches on her own, as well as reporting her ideas for the new clients to Mr. Carlson.

She'd gone home exhausted each night and fielded questions from Milo as to whether she'd heard from Stephen or not. He'd only called twice so far, and the first time Milo had been asleep since it was past his bedtime. The second night, Milo was still at Karen's while Madison had worked late finishing up a proposal for the executives meeting with her the next day.

She'd texted him a list of good times to call, and he'd only replied with a thank you and nothing more.

On Thursday, her phone rang, and when she recognized the number as Stephen's, she handed the phone to Milo to answer, too tired and bitter to deal with the man. Milo talked to him for a few minutes then asked her if Saturday would be a good day for the zoo.

She nodded sleepily, and Milo spoke into the phone. "She said yes." He listened for a moment then turned to her. "He wants to know if you want to come."

Madison debated for a moment, but the idea of walking around a zoo on the only day she had off didn't sound appealing. "No, buddy, I don't think so."

"She said, no. So it's just us." Milo seemed eager, and Madison wondered how Stephen had reacted to the news. Milo hung up the phone and passed it back to her then left for his room, mumbling something about needing to find his book on lions so he could read up about them before he saw them again.

Madison stared at the phone in her hand, contemplating on calling him back. She wanted to hear his voice, to know what he was up to, but he hadn't asked to speak with her, and she would leave it at that. She could see him Saturday if she wanted. Or avoid him all together.

If only she knew which she wanted more. She set the phone on the dresser and went to take a long shower.

Stephen set the phone down, disappointed he hadn't been able to talk to Madison. He'd been surprised to hear Milo answer the phone, but it was good to talk to the kid. He missed him and couldn't wait to get this job done so he could return to California. But the consulting fee on this account would make it possible for him to take some time off once it was completed, so he could pursue Madison full-time.

He'd had her back in his life for just a short time, but she'd worked her way into his heart so deep he knew he couldn't let her go again. And with Milo cementing them together in a way he didn't know was possible, he longed to make them a family. Milo would be all for it, but Madison would take some tender care. He had his past to overcome.

He stared at the phone, realizing he'd just done the same thing. Left her during a time of stress and upheaval in her life. He pressed the button to call her, needing to speak with her, to assure her he wanted to stay in touch, that he wouldn't be gone forever and would return if she'd have him. But the phone just rang until it went to voicemail.

He didn't dare leave a message, not knowing what to say without coming off as a rambling idiot. He turned it off then sent a text instead.

I miss you.

He hoped to see a response, but nothing came.

He leaned his head against the back of the hotel chair. He'd screwed up good this time and hoped she wouldn't take him leaving for a job as an indication he didn't care about her.

He worked long hours each day, hoping to get things wrapped up as soon as possible so he could return and see her in person. She'd obviously avoided his phone calls, either by letting them go to voicemail during the workday or by passing the phone to Milo in the evenings when he called. At least she let him speak to the boy.

He sent texts daily, asking about work, asking about Milo, asking about how the weather was, trying to get some kind of response from her, but they were never answered. The silent treatment was eating at him, but he persevered. He even ordered an exotic blend of tropical flowers to be delivered to her at work and hoped they would help when he returned.

Saturday morning, Stephen headed to the airport, and when he reached the on-ramp for the freeway, he groaned and turned on the local news radio. A multi-car accident had the freeway backed up for hours, and it would be almost impossible to make it to the airport in time to make his flight, given all the traffic overflowing onto the side streets.

He called the airline and checked on his flight to see if he could change to a later one, but they had no openings until later in the afternoon, which would put him too late to take Milo to the zoo today.

"Would you like me to transfer your seat?" the woman on the phone asked.

"How many seats do you have?"

"One moment." Stephen could hear sounds on the other end of the phone, then she came back on. "I'm sorry, sir, but it seems like that flight has just been booked full. We do have openings for tomorrow."

Stephen heaved a breath of frustration. "I'll look into it and call you back. Thank you for your help." He hung up the phone and called Madison's number. It rang a few times, then her groggy voice came on. Crap, he'd woken her up.

"Hello?"

"Madison, hi. Sorry to wake you. I've got bad news. I can't make my flight today and will need to reschedule with Milo. Can you tell him?"

"What?" Her voice sounded a little more alert.

"I can't make my flight back to California. I will need to reschedule the zoo with Milo." He inched the rental car forward on the freeway, trying to merge onto the road so he could get to the next off-ramp and get out of the traffic mess. "I hate to do this, but it really isn't my fault."

Madison's voice was flat. "It never is. Look, don't bother letting your son get in the way of your life. He's done fine without you so far. I'm sure he can manage without you again."

"That's not fair," Stephen said.

"Life isn't fair, Stephen," Madison replied. "Get over it and move on. We did."

She hung up the phone, and Stephen swore. He hit the redial button, but she wouldn't answer him.

"Fine, be that way. But you won't keep me from seeing Milo."

He called the airline back and scheduled a flight for Sunday morning then sent a message to his client that he would need to take a couple personal days at the beginning of the week but would keep in touch through emails and Skype. He wouldn't let this setback keep him down long.

He needed to do some planning and figure out a way to get back into her good graces, at least for Milo's sake, even if she really didn't want anything to do with him. He would not abandon his son.

Chapter Twenty-eight

Stephen knocked on the door to Madison's house Sunday mid-morning. Her car was not in her driveway, so maybe she was gone. He texted her, hoping at least it would go through.

We need to talk. I'm at your house.

He watched the little bubble on his phone indicating she was responding. Finally. When the answer came through, he scowled.

Lucky for me, I'm not.

Her words stung, and he struggled with what to say. He couldn't antagonize her, but he wanted to tell her off. He breathed slowly for a bit, staring at his car against the curb. He sat down on her steps, ready to wait for her.

What do you want? She asked after a moment.

I have a commitment to keep with Milo. I'd like to take him to the zoo today if he's available. He paused then sent a follow-up message. *You don't have to come if you don't want. I can handle being the parent.*

The bubbles indicating she was texting him stopped, and he waited for her response.

The bubbles started again and she replied. *We'll be back in an hour. You can either wait there, or I could drop him off at the zoo, and you can meet him at the front gate.*

The zoo would be great. See you there.

Stephen tucked his phone in his pocket and headed to his car. It would take him probably thirty minutes or more to get to the zoo. If they met there, it would allow him more time with Milo. This wasn't the perfect solution, but it would work for now.

He made his way to the front gate, debating on buying two or three admittance tickets. He didn't want to force Madison to come, and it would make for an awkward date if she didn't want to be there. He decided to wait and see how things went when they arrived. As he waited, he pulled out his phone and did a few business things and was happy to see the new client wasn't hounding him with frivolous emails.

"Dad!" Milo's little voice called out, and Stephen lifted his head. Milo ran toward him wearing the little backpack he always had with him and grabbed Stephen in a big hug. He gripped the kid tightly and lifted him off the ground.

"Hey, kiddo." Stephen looked up to see Madison

standing near the curb on the sidewalk by her car. She hadn't parked and walked over, but had just dropped him off, indicating she didn't want to be with them.

He waved at her. "Thanks."

Milo looked at her then back to him. "She said she wants me home by seven."

"Seven." Stephen nodded, looking into Milo's face. "Got it." He turned his attention back to Madison. "Seven, it is."

She nodded then walked around her car without another word to him. Is this where they were now? Communicating through their child? How did he let it get to this?

"Thanks for coming back. I didn't think we'd be able to do it. I can't wait to go see the lions. Can we go in now?"

Stephen set him down and took his hand as they walked over to the ticket counter.

Madison pulled away, and as she took the turn around the parking lot toward the exit, she couldn't help watching the two dark heads leaning toward each other as they talked. Milo looked small in Stephen's arms, just like a little boy should when being held by the father he adored.

As angry as she was at Stephen for abandoning her again, she couldn't keep the two of them apart. Milo had been so disappointed that Stephen had called to postpone again. When she'd told him about the text from Stephen earlier that day, he'd shouted with excitement and begged to leave right away to go meet him. Part of her wished she could have gone with them to watch them together and see how good they were for each other.

But she'd over reacted again when he'd canceled. She didn't blame him for just ignoring her and spending his attention on Milo. It was how it should be. Milo needed his dad more than she needed a man.

Stephen had a blast. He couldn't remember ever enjoying the zoo more than he did with Milo. They'd seen everything there was to see and had returned to the lion exhibit twice. Milo had been so enamored with the animal that Stephen bought one of the stuffed lions at the little gift shop next to the enclosure.

Milo named it Claw, and Stephen smiled. At least it wasn't Liony like he would have done at that age.

As they drove home, Milo fell asleep in the back

seat, holding the stuffed lion close. Hopefully, it would help him remember his dad while they were apart for now. He wished he could have talked to Milo about Madison but didn't think it was the right time to pester the boy for details about his mother. Besides, he didn't want to hear about what she'd said to Milo about him.

When he pulled up at her house, the front porch light was on, and though it wasn't dark, the sun would be setting before long. He was late and wondered how much trouble he'd be in for not getting Milo home by seven. The traffic had been bad for a Sunday evening, and they'd gone to get something for dinner after the zoo closed at six.

But if he was in trouble with her, at least he'd scored some points with Milo. He opened the door, poked his head into the back seat, and gently shook Milo awake. "Hey, kiddo, we're home."

Milo struggled to wake up but leaned his head back against the seat. He must have overdone it. Stephen made sure Milo had ahold of Claw and his backpack, picked the boy up out of the car, then kicked the door closed with his foot.

When he reached the front door, Madison opened it without him even needing to knock. She raised her eyebrow.

"Sorry, guess we just didn't know when to quit." Stephen adjusted Milo over his shoulder a little better.

She stepped back, and Stephen entered the house. "Should I just take him to his room?" Stephen asked.

She nodded, so Stephen carried him into the room. Madison's phone rang, and Stephen watched as she turned around and answered the call.

"Hey, Momma. How are you?"

Stephen's gut clenched. She was talking to her mother. Did Lorna know he was back in her daughter's life? He stood frozen in Milo's room after laying the boy on his bed. His hope for a moment of privacy with Madison wouldn't go over well tonight. He stepped out of the room and walked down the hallway to see Madison's back turned to him as she stood in her kitchen talking to her mother.

He let himself out, not wanting to interrupt. He would have to figure out another way to get her alone.

Madison took a slow breath. She loved her mother, she really did, but the woman had called at the wrong time. She needed to talk to Stephen. She had to set things right.

"Mom, I don't have a lot of time to talk right now. Can I call you back?"

"Oh, right. Sorry dear. Yeah, you can call back, but

I did want to let you know Dad and I were thinking of taking a trip to see you guys."

"You're coming here?"

"Yes. Dad's done the last of the bailing this season, and he wanted to make a trip to the coast then head up and see the Redwoods. We wanted to know if you and Milo wanted to take a trip with us."

Madison pinched the bridge of her nose. "That sounds fun, but I just got promoted at work, and I've got a lot on my plate right now. I'd love for you to stop and see us, of course, but I don't think I can take the time off work right now."

"That's great, honey. You deserve a promotion. You're so good at what you do."

"Thanks, Mom."

"What about Milo? Maybe we could take him with us. Give you a break. Being a single parent has to be tough. I don't know how you do it."

Madison took a slow breath. Her mother had often remarked on how brave she'd been to do this alone, but now, it just reminded her of how much she'd lost because of listening to her parents' advice. "We can talk about it later, Mom. I've got to go. Text me the dates so I can see if there's anything Milo can't miss."

"Will do. Have a good night, Beatrice." Her mother still refused to call her Madison, but since she was the one who'd named her, she got a few more privileges than others would.

"Night, Mom." Madison hung up the phone and turned around to go find Stephen. When she entered Milo's room, she wasn't surprised Stephen wasn't there, but as she entered the front room, she realized he had left without a word. Was it really only about Milo for him, or was she blowing her chance?

Madison sank into the couch and stared at the black screen of her television, empty and just as dark as the cloud that had settled over her soul.

Chapter Twenty-nine

Stephen returned to Oregon on Monday, though he had planned to stay in California for the first part of the week. He didn't dare press his luck and ask for a few more days with Milo. Not after having returned him home late on their first outing, the same night her mom had called. Madison had probably told her mom all about his irresponsibility, making a mountain out of a molehill.

And with the call he'd gotten from his client, he knew he could get their project wrapped up quicker if he returned in person. Fast enough that he could probably be back home by Friday. Then he'd take some time off work to make his case to Madison.

He worked like mad during the day, calling Milo in the evenings, not surprised anymore when he answered Madison's phone. At least the calls went through and she hadn't blocked him.

"How was your day, Milo?" Stephen asked on their Wednesday call.

"Good."

"Do anything fun?"

"Yeah, played with Legos."

They talked about the Legos for a few minutes, then Stephen asked what his plans were for the last couple weeks of summer. He'd be starting school soon, and Stephen hoped to be settled in the area so he could be a part of it.

"Grandma and Grandpa Perry are going to take me on a trip to the Redwoods."

Stephen stopped chewing the food in his mouth. He rearranged it to the side and asked. "How long? Is your mom going too?"

"No, Mom said she had to work."

Stephen considered that for a moment. Were Milo's grandparents trying to keep him from Stephen? Had it been their idea, or had Madison done this? "How long is the trip for?" he asked again.

"I think it's for a week. Not sure. Should I go ask Mom?"

"No, that's okay. I hope you have a fun trip. When do you leave?"

"Next week."

Stephen nodded, though Milo couldn't see him. He wouldn't have Milo there as an excuse to see

Madison, but maybe it would give him a chance to show her that he wasn't just in it for the kid. But she wouldn't see him without Milo. He needed a way to talk to her where she couldn't get away.

"I'll be coming back tomorrow night. Would you like to go do something?"

"Yeah. We could go to the park. Mom doesn't have much time lately."

"Is she still really busy at work?" Stephen asked.

"Yeah." A few noises in the background made Stephen think Milo was playing with Legos as they talked. "It must be really hard 'cause sometimes she cries at night after dinner."

Stephen held the phone tighter to his ear. "Is she there in the room with you?" He paused, not thinking he should ask Milo if he thought she was sad because of something different.

"No, she's watching a movie."

"I'm sorry your mom is sad. I think I might know something to help her feel better. Do you think you might help me cheer her up?" Stephen asked. He hesitated for a moment, not sure if this idea would backfire or not, but he was desperate enough to enlist the help of a seven-year-old.

Madison stared at Milo Thursday night as she tried to tuck him into bed. "You've got to be kidding me. You left it in the car?"

"Sorry, Mom. I forgot Claw when we came in. And I can't sleep without him. Please."

Milo's eyes were huge, and she didn't understand what was so important about the stupid stuffed animal anyway. It wasn't as if he'd had it long. Stephen had bought it for him at the zoo last week. She dropped her shoulders in defeat and sighed.

"Fine. I'll go get it."

"I'll come help you find him." Milo threw the covers off and shot past her into the hallway. She was half-tempted to just let him run out to the car himself, but he was still pretty young, and though her neighborhood was relatively safe, she still didn't feel comfortable letting him go alone.

He'd left the front door open in his rush out there. She grabbed the keys from her purse and hurried down the driveway after him.

Milo ran back to her. "Can I open it?"

Madison passed the keys over to him, and he pressed the button, running closer to the back door. He kept the keys in his hand, opened his door, and peered in. "I can't see it."

Madison rolled her eyes. "It's on the floor against

the other door."

"Where?" Milo said, not even looking in the car.

Madison shook her head, not wanting to argue with him. It was easier to just do it herself. She stepped into the car so she could reach it and felt Milo push her from behind.

"Hey!" she hollered. "What are you—" The door closed behind her, and Madison turned to glare at her son. She tried opening the door, but with the child-locks on, it wouldn't open and she wasn't in the mood to climb into the front seat. She pointed her finger at him. "Open this door, Milo."

Milo wasn't even looking at her, but was waving to someone behind the car. Madison looked through the back windshield and frowned when she saw Stephen approaching her car.

He opened the front door and climbed in then turned to face her. Madison glared at him then back to her son who lifted the car keys and pressed the lock button. He waved at Stephen, gave him a thumbs up, and ran into the house, closing the door behind him.

"What the heck is this all about?" Madison asked. "Did you put him up to this?"

Stephen shrugged. "I merely suggested I needed a moment to talk to you. And since you won't meet with me, or see me, or even talk to me on the phone anymore now that we no longer work together, I thought I'd enlist the help of our son."

"My son is going to be in some big trouble." Madison looked back at the door, not wanting to even look at Stephen.

"My son is doing exactly what I asked," Stephen said. "I think that deserves some praise."

"He's not your son. You may be his biological father, but you are not his dad." Madison snapped.

Stephen sighed. "Maybe you should be a little more careful what you say right now. Don't want you to regret anything."

"There are a lot of things I regret." Madison crossed her arms over her chest and stared at him. She regretted so much about this man and the time she had wasted on him. If she hadn't pined away after him for so long, she might have let herself find someone else. If she hadn't listened to the advice from her parents, she might have had these last eight years with him. If she hadn't gotten so angry at everything he'd done or said, she wouldn't be feeling so uncomfortable to be with him right now.

"Me too." Stephen turned to look at her, leaning his arm across the seat so he could face her better. His large body filled the front half of the car, and she leaned against the back window, trying to stay as far away from him as possible. "I regret not coming back to find you. I regret letting your parents scare me away.

I regret not being here for Milo all these years. I regret leaving Carlson's so abruptly, but I thought you needed space. I regret kissing you and scaring you away that night we watched the movie. I should have controlled myself better, but instead I let my desire for you cloud my judgment.

"But there is one thing I don't regret." Stephen stared at her. "I don't regret loving you. And though you may not want to hear this, I need to tell you. You are exactly what I've been looking for all my life. The mother of my child. The one who raised him all on her own and turned him into the amazing kid he is. The one who stole my heart the moment I laid eyes on you again. I was an idiot before. I had feelings for you, but I didn't do it right. I allowed myself to get lost in the moment, then the next minute I was gone and didn't come back when things got hard. Then I did almost the same kind of thing this time around. That was wrong of me, and I regret it more than anything."

Madison stared at him, the anger subsiding to a painful sadness. They'd lost so much time, and if she wasn't careful, she would push him away completely. He would stay for Milo, for sure, but if things didn't work out with her, that would hurt too much when he left again.

"Madison, I don't want to do it this way. I wanted to be a part of your life. And if you want it to just be

214

by seeing Milo every few days, then I'll accept that. But you need to know how I feel about you."

Madison kept her mouth closed, not willing to say anything yet. Not knowing what to say. She still felt so much anger at him leaving again.

Madison stared at him. She wished he weren't so far away. She wanted to wrap her arms around him and hold him tight. To feel his arms encircle her and make everything feel better, but she still didn't trust herself. She needed time to think without him staring her down.

"Let me out," Madison said. "Please."

Stephen met her eyes, apparently searching for something. He turned and let out a slow breath. "All right." He got out of the car and pulled her door open.

Stephen looked into Madison's eyes, seeing the sadness filling them to the brim with tears. "Let me out, please," she said.

He couldn't keep her in here forever. Holding her against her will wasn't going to help him win her over. He let out a slow breath. "All right." He hit the unlock button and climbed out of the car then looked at the house. Through the gap in the curtains, Stephen could make out Milo's face peeking through. He hated to think he was going to disappoint his son. But he had years to work on Madison. Maybe eventually she would warm up to him.

He would go slow and take all the time needed until she forgave him.

He pulled her door open and stepped back so she had room to move. Madison's pajama-clad leg was soon followed by the second one. She stood up and looked at him then pushed the door closed. He watched her as she stood in front of him, staring up into his face.

She took one step forward and wrapped her arms around his middle, placing her head against his chest in a hug. He was shocked at first, unsure what she was doing, but as she held him there, he lifted his hands from his side and slowly wrapped them around her. She nestled in closer to him, squeezing him tighter, and he held her close.

It felt like a hug goodbye, and his heart ached. He was losing her, and there was nothing he could do about it without making her run harder and farther from him. He allowed himself to hold her as long as she'd let him. Maybe this would sustain him for a while.

She loosened her hold on him and pulled back just a little. He reluctantly released her, expecting her to turn and walk away into the house, but instead she wrapped her arms around herself and looked up into his face.

"I'm sorry," Madison said. "I've done this all wrong, and I don't know what to do now. I'm no good at any of this."

He lifted his hands and pressed a finger against her lips to stop her words. He moved his hands until they cupped the sides of her face, his thumbs wiping away the tears that stained her cheeks.

"I'm sorry too," Stephen said.

"I want to give this a chance, but I'm so scared," Madison said. She took a slow breath and pulled his hands away from her face. "I need time. And it's late tonight."

Stephen nodded. "Can I see you tomorrow?"

"I have to work late, but why don't you and Milo do something. I'll have Karen text you her address and you can let her know what time you'll get Milo. I'll call you when I'm done. We can go from there."

"I can accept that. Thank you."

Madison stepped away from him and returned to her house. Milo opened the door, his head partly down as if expecting to be in trouble.

Madison looked at him for a moment then nodded her head back toward the car. "You go get your own lion."

Milo's gaze met Stephen's looking confused and

unsure. He jogged toward the car and Stephen ruffled his hair. "Thanks, kiddo."

"Is Mom going to be happy now?" Milo asked.

"Some day. We're trying to work things out, but we'll figure out the best thing for all of us. She has to work late tomorrow, you want to do something with me? I have to do some phone calls in the morning, but I can come pick you up around one."

Milo nodded. "Okay."

"Museum?" Stephen asked.

"I guess." Milo climbed into the car and grabbed his stuffed lion.

"We can go out to eat afterward too," Stephen said, and Milo smiled, looking a little more excited.

"Milo," Madison called from the front door. "It's time to get to bed."

Milo looked back up at Stephen. "See you tomorrow, Dad."

Stephen watched the two most important people in his life disappear into the house without him, and he hoped eventually to join them.

Chapter Thirty

$\mathcal{A}$s they left the museum and headed to the car, Milo asked, "Can we get something to eat?"

"Sure, kiddo. Where do you want to go?" Stephen rattled off a few of the sit-down restaurants nearby and Milo picked one.

"Mom never takes me to that one."

Stephen smiled. "Then we'd better go there."

The wait time wasn't long and they chatted happily while waiting for the food. It was nice to not just get a burger or chicken nuggets like they'd done most times. And they'd have time to eat and still get him home by eight. Madison would probably be home by then, and they could begin to work things out.

As the waitress put the food in front of them, Milo tucked into it like he'd been starving and Stephen did the same. He speared his shrimp scampi with a fork and Milo studied Stephen's plate. "What's that, Dad?"

"Shrimp. Want to try?" Stephen held out the fork and Milo shrugged. "Have you ever tried shrimp before?"

Milo shook his head. "Don't think so."

"It's good. Here."

Milo took the fork and bit carefully into the curved part of the shrimp. He chewed gingerly and swallowed. "It tastes weird." Milo handed the fork back without finishing the entire shrimp and Stephen chuckled.

"No worries, you can slowly get used to it. I love it."

Milo brought his hand to his mouth and wiped it, then took a bite of his mac and cheese and chewed slowly, reaching up and rubbing his lip again. He swallowed and took a drink. "My mouth itches."

Stephen passed him his unused napkin dipped in his water glass. "Wipe the cheese sauce off your face."

Milo scrubbed his face and when he put the napkin down, Stephen frowned at the swollen bottom lip.

"Milo, are you having an allergic reaction?"

Milo's eyes widened as he reached up and touched his lips. "I don't have my epi-pen. I left my backpack at Aunt Karen's."

Stephen stood up and moved around the table to Milo. "What do we do?"

"Call Mom."

Stephen pulled out his phone and frantically dialed Madison. It just rang, then went to voice-mail. Stephen grunted in frustration and left a message. "Call me, now!" He grabbed his wallet and pulled out a few twenties, hoping he'd guessed the right price and threw them on the table. Gripping Milo's hand, he rushed out of the restaurant, trying to explain to the hostess that he had to get the kid to the hospital.

By the time they'd gotten into the car, Milo's face was completely flushed and his lips were swollen to twice the size. Small looking blisters were forming near his eyes and all over his cheeks and Stephen panicked. "Get buckled! We're heading to the ER."

The few minutes it took to get to the hospital were the longest and worst in all of Stephen's life. He kept talking to Milo, telling him it would be okay, making him answer questions and keep a running commentary on his symptoms. As he pulled into the spot just for ambulances at the ER doors, Stephen threw the car into park and jumped out, yanking the back door open and grabbing Milo in a football hold and sprinting through the doors.

"He ate some shrimp, and is having a reaction!"

The nurses took him into a curtained room and started asking him questions, then another nurse took Stephen to the side to ask him questions he didn't know how to answer. He didn't know how much he weighed, what other things he was allergic to besides tree nuts or if he'd ever had a shell-fish reaction before, or anything about his medical history.

A paramedic rushed through the doors, shouting for the idiot who was blocking the ambulance to move their car and Stephen ran out to take care of that.

He tried calling Madison again after parking as he jogged back to the hospital doors, but the phone just rang again. He texted her, hoping she didn't panic when she read the words ER and allergy. Things went by in a blur. Milo was treated and his face no longer looked as swollen, making Stephen relax just a little. Madison finally called and Stephen was grateful he'd be able to report Milo was on the mend.

"Where are you!" she shouted into the phone as soon as Stephen answered. He gave her the information about which hospital. "I'll be there in ten minutes." She hung up without saying another word.

Stephen paced the little curtained room, not looking forward to seeing Madison after almost killing their son. She would never trust him now or give him a chance after this.

Madison rushed through the ER doors and grabbed the first nurse she could find. "My son's here. Allergy. Milo Perry."

The nurse led her back to a curtained area and Milo's happy face smiled up at her. "Mom!"

Madison hurried over to him where he sat propped up on the gurney and gave him a hug. "Milo, I was so worried about you, what happened? What did you eat?" She turned to Stephen. "Did you give him something with nuts? How could this happen?" She turned back to Milo. "Where was your backpack? You know you're supposed to keep it with you at all times. This could happen with anything made in a factory with nuts."

She turned back to Stephen. "You should have been more careful. Did you read the package? What did you give him?"

The look of devastation on Stephen's face stopped her tirade for a moment. He opened his mouth to speak, but Milo beat him to it. "Mom, calm down. It wasn't a nut."

Madison looked between the two, then sat on the edge of Milo's bed. "What was it?"

"Shrimp," Stephen said. "I didn't know. You never told me he could have any allergies to shell fish."

Madison looked at Milo again. "You ate shrimp?" He had never wanted to try it when she ordered it. Why would he eat it now? "I didn't know he had a shell fish allergy."

Milo nodded. "Yeah, the doctor said sometimes it happens with people who have nut allergies. Said I'll have to be careful with regular fish too." He sounded so grown up for a seven year old and she was relieved he was so calm about this. He hadn't had a life threatening reaction for years and they'd become too comfortable. "But Dad got me here fast enough for them to give me the shot."

"I'm so glad you're okay." She hugged him again then stood up and moved over to Stephen. It was hard to meet his eyes, but she knew she had to apologize. To make it right between them. She had over reacted big time and accused him of carelessness when it wasn't his fault.

"I'm sorry I yelled at you. Thank you, Stephen. For taking care of our boy." She took his hand, hoping he wouldn't pull back in anger like he had every right to do.

"I'm sorry, Madison. I had no idea. It happened so fast and I was so worried I'd hurt him."

Madison heard the same terror in his voice she had felt the first time they'd discovered Milo's allergy. "Sounds like you did everything right." Madison stepped closer and slid her arms around him for a hug. "Thank you." She held him for a few minutes until the

ER doctor came in and gave them some final instructions before discharging them.

"Milo will probably be tired, but you need to make sure you keep giving him regular doses of the antihistamine." The doctor circled the dosage on the papers he held. "Keep an eye on him, because if the shot wears off before the allergen is out of his system, he could have another reaction. And you'll need to do a follow up with an allergist."

Madison nodded and from Stephen's body language, she knew he was listening closely to the instructions as well. It was obvious he loved Milo as much as she did. When they were sure they knew what to do, the doctor left. Milo climbed off the gurney just as a nurse came in. She looked at Stephen. "Are you the person responsible for payment?"

Madison stepped forward and lifted her purse to dig out her wallet. "That would be me."

Milo looked at his mom. "Can I ride home with Dad?"

Madison hesitated for a moment, but nodded and smiled at Stephen. "Is that okay with you? This might take a few minutes."

He nodded, but looked at Milo as he answered, not meeting her eye. "Sure. We'll see you at your house."

Milo looked about ready to fall asleep as Stephen pulled up to his house. They got out of the car and Stephen offered to carry him to the door. Milo lifted his arms and Stephen picked up his son, reveling in the fierce hug the boy gave him, glad he was okay. When they reached the front door, Stephen paused.

"Do you have a key, Milo?"

He shook his head drowsily against Stephen's shoulder. Stephen sighed then turned around on the porch and took a couple steps down. He eased Milo out of the monkey hold he had on him and they sat on the steps to wait for Madison.

She pulled up about ten minutes later and rushed out of the car. "I'm so sorry, I didn't even think about the house being locked. I should have given you my keys. Why didn't you call me?"

Stephen shrugged. "It was nice to just sit here with Milo."

Madison looked at him, then at the sleepy boy leaning on his shoulder. She didn't speak, but moved past them to unlock the house. Stephen helped Milo stand and they entered the house soon after Madison.

"I'm hungry, Mom."

"There's some yogurt and apples in the fridge, go

pick out something that sounds good."

Milo headed to the kitchen and Stephen stared after the boy, afraid to let him out of his sight.

"Terrifying, isn't it?" Madison slid up beside him and took his hand in hers.

"I had no idea," Stephen said, glancing down at her.

"I was afraid to let him do anything for days, and I checked labels religiously, made sure I had an epi-pen in my purse, in the kitchen, in my room, in the bathroom, in the car. Everywhere. Made him carry around a little backpack too. Which I'm surprised he didn't have with him."

"I'm sorry, I should have made sure he had it. I know he has it with him all the time. He was just excited to see me, so I didn't even—" He stopped short when Madison stepped in front of him.

"It's okay." Madison sighed. "You did fine. Much better than I did the first time. Milo will be good as new in a few days, and now we know to stay away from shrimp. It's all good."

Stephen took a deep breath, finally feeling a little more at ease. She truly didn't blame him for this and it gave him hope.

Madison looked up into his eyes. "Besides. It made me realize how much I want you to be a more permanent part of Milo's life." She took a slow breath.

"And mine."

"Really?" Stephen wasn't sure if he was actually hearing this right.

Madison pulled back and wiped her eyes. "I keep messing up, Stephen. I've been on my own so long and in charge of everything, I don't know when to stop. And I was so afraid of you leaving again that I just pushed you away first so I wouldn't get hurt. But I don't want to do it alone anymore. Not if I don't have to."

Stephen didn't know what to say. He'd been so afraid of moving too fast.

"We don't have to be an immediate family, Stephen," Madison continued. "We can take our time. I'm here. You're here. Milo is with us both. We can become a family when it's right, but I won't—"

Stephen took her hands in his. "I don't want to leave you. If you'll let me stay, I will."

Madison's smile warmed his heart. He bent his head, and she lifted her face toward him. Their eyes remained locked on each other's until he was so close he could feel her warm breath on his skin. She closed her eyes in that sexy way she had, and his heart pounded in his chest. He closed his eyes and pressed his lips to hers, wanting to enjoy every second of this kiss.

She sighed softly against his lips and moved her

arms around his neck, pressing her body close to his. He let go of her hands, and one of his found its way around her back while the other cradled the back of her head.

She kissed him back, putting more passion and emotion into this than he'd felt from her since finding her again. Then, too soon, she ended the kiss and sobbed against him.

Her shoulders shook as she cried. Stephen held her, more confused than ever. He'd never made a woman cry with his kisses, and from what he could tell from before, she'd enjoyed them. He rubbed her back and made soothing sounds, hoping she'd calm down enough to tell him what to do.

"Bea, love, don't cry. We'll figure it out."

Madison sighed. "I know. I'm not crying because I'm sad. I'm crying because I'm so happy to have you here with me right now. I hated doing all this parenting stuff alone. It's nice to have a dad in the house."

"Does this mean Dad will be moving in with us?" Milo asked from the hallway making Stephen and Madison pull apart in surprise.

"Maybe someday, Milo," Stephen said. "But first I need to ask your mom to marry me."

"Then ask her," Milo said before taking a bite of his apple.

Stephen looked down into Madison's face,

searching it for any clue to her thoughts on the subject. She smiled at him, then lifted up on her toes and kissed him softly. She whispered against his lips. "Don't feel pressured to ask, if you aren't ready. But I kinda think if you did ask, the answer would be yes."

Stephen smiled, then looked over at Milo who smiled wide and nodded eagerly. Stephen kept hold of Madison's hand and led her over to the orchids he'd brought over weeks ago. The blossoms were still full and vibrant. It wasn't a typical Hawaiian flower, but it would do in a pinch. He pulled the blossom off and bent down on one knee, holding the flower up. "Beatrice Madison Perry, will you do me the honor of allowing me to be your husband?"

She leaned down toward him. "You're sure?"

"Of course I'm sure. I want us to be a family. I've already missed too much of it, I don't want to waste a moment more." He held one hand out to Milo who joined them. "Milo, is it okay with you if I marry your mom?"

"Yup."

Madison smiled at Milo then looked back at Stephen. "Then yes, I'd love to marry you."

Stephen stood and tucked the blossom behind her left ear, officially declaring her taken, then kissed her gently.

Milo grinned and hugged them both. "Finally."

Stephen chuckled. "My thoughts exactly, son."

Epilogue

Stephen stood at the one end of the chapel watching his bride walk toward him. She had her hand tucked into her father's elbow. The last few months had been a time of closure and forgiveness. It had been hard to meet with Madison's parents after they'd come back with Milo from their trip to the Redwoods, but over time, they had begun to accept him as a part of Madison and Milo's lives.

Stephen glanced at his son in his tux, standing next to him as his best man. Milo grinned up at him, and he turned his attention back to Madison. She didn't have a veil covering her face, just a single plumeria flower over her right ear. He stared at her bright eyes shining with the same joy he felt.

It was a long time coming, but they would finally be a family. When Madison reached him, she leaned over and kissed her father on the cheek.

Joe paused, took her hand in his one last time, kissed her knuckles, and passed her hand into Stephen's. Joe smiled at him without any trace of sadness, and Stephen returned the smile, then focused all his attention on the woman before him.

They turned to the officiator, and as they said the words that would unite them as a family, Stephen's heart swelled within him.

"I now pronounce you husband and wife. You may kiss the bride."

Stephen kissed her as tenderly as he could, breathing in her scent and looking forward to the promise of more moments like this. He took the flower and moved it to the other side, and she grinned widely.

As they walked down the aisle as a married couple, Madison leaned in closer to him. "Are you going to tell me now where we're going on our honeymoon?"

He glanced at her as they walked. "Surely you've got some ideas."

Madison smiled. "Well, I'm hoping you're smart enough to take me to Hawaii like you promised to do once upon a time."

His grin nearly split his face. "I have tickets for tomorrow. But for tonight I didn't want to be on the red-eye."

Madison smiled. "Smart thinking. I have other plans for tonight as well." She squeezed his arm, and they walked outside and into the waiting limo.

Dear Reader,

I hope you enjoyed reading *Echoes of Summer*. Please consider posting a review or rating on Amazon or Goodreads. Reviews help spread the word. It's the best way to say "thank you" to any author.

If you have questions or comments, please feel free to contact me at authorlaurabastian@gmail.com.
Find me on:
www.lauradbastian.com
www.facebook.com/AuthorLauraBastian

Thanks for reading.

Laura D. Bastian

Acknowledgments

So many people go into the creation of a book, from the person who sparks the idea, to the friends who let me pester them asking for help, advice, tips, and so much more. I want to thank Kirsten Osbourne for the mentoring and help through this story. Lindzee Armstrong for help and tips in formatting and revisions. Cindy Whitney for the encouragement, brainstorming, beta reads, and links for advice on writing romance as well as more formatting tips and her mad skills at images. Jaclyn Weist for checking up on me and helping this happen in a timely manner. And to my chat room buddies in the Sprintwriters Central website for the cheer leading.

And as always, thanks to my husband and children who tolerate my absence when I'm totally immersed in writing and revisions and who only roll their eyes just a little when I tell them, no this story doesn't have any magic in it. Just kissing.

About Laura D. Bastian

Laura grew up in a small town in central Utah and now lives in another small town in northern Utah. She always loved stargazing and imagining life out-side her own little world. A graduate of Utah State University with a degree in Elementary and Special Education, Laura has been using that training as she raises her children and writes make believe worlds. You can usually find her on her laptop either typing away, or on social media interacting with friends when she's not playing in her garden.

Sneak Peek of
Sink or Swim

A HIDDEN IDENTITIES ANTHOLOGY NOVELLA

LAURA D. BASTIAN

Chapter One

*S*helly pulled off her teacher badge and smiled. The school day was over, and it was time to head to the pool for her daily laps. If she hurried the minute her contract hours were over, she could make it before the afternoon rush started and have the pool to herself. One of the good things about starting the school day so early.

She hopped in her dad's old convertible Mustang he'd given her as a college graduation gift and drove the four blocks to her gym. She relished the warm sun on her skin, knowing it wouldn't be long before the weather turned cool. Thoughts of the warm climate of Africa reminded her of her broken plans. She would have been there with Charlie right now if she hadn't caught him with another woman a few weeks before their wedding.

It had been four months since she'd kicked him to

the curb, and though she would have loved to have been in Africa on a humanitarian project, she knew she could still do a lot of good right in her own neighborhood.

The locker room at the gym was nearly empty, and she nodded politely at a woman passing her on the way to the showers. Within thirty minutes, the locker room would be crowded and noisy. Shelly changed into her plain black suit, cut high at the neck and low on the legs, then grabbed her towel and headed to her escape. She breathed in the humid air filled with the familiar scent of chlorine.

The corners of her mouth turned down when she saw that her favorite lane was occupied. Though there were three other lanes, she wanted hers. She sighed heavily and glanced at the clock. Could she wait him out? It was definitely a him. A nice looking him at that. She had no idea how long he'd been there, but the definition of his muscles and the power of his strokes testified of years spent doing laps.

She decided not to wait, tossed her towel on the bench, and began her pre-swim stretches. The man continued to swim without noticing her at all, so she adjusted her goggles, made sure her swim cap was tight and dove in. As soon as she hit the water, all the stresses washed away. Even the annoyance of a man in her pool. She pushed herself, zeroing in on the pressure of the water as it brushed against her skin with each stroke. After doing her customary ten laps of the front crawl, she shifted easily into the breast stroke for another ten laps. As she transitioned into the back stroke, she knew she was being watched.

From the corner of her eye she saw the man toweling off on the edge of the pool. His swim shorts were snug and hung low on his hips with the weight of the water. Thank goodness it wasn't a Speedo. In her experience, guys who wore those were always extra annoying. His washboard abs caught her eye and her concentration broke. She forced herself to ignore him and continue her laps. As she passed him once more on her return lap, she was both relieved and disappointed to see he was moving away from the pool's edge.

That's strange. Most guys wanted to talk while she tried to swim. *How refreshing.*

Her mind wandered to the man, and she struggled to stay focused on her strokes. *Get over it, Shelly. Men aren't worth it.* She forced thoughts of her ex-fiancé out of her mind and swam harder, pushing herself to the point where she couldn't feel anything besides the rhythm of her strokes. Even the water had disappeared for a moment, and she was content just to exist in a state of limbo.

***

Brandon had come to the pool on a whim, hoping to find a way to ease some of the tension caused by the move back home. Swimming had done the trick, loosening him up enough he figured he could handle another visit with his parents. He made enough money to afford his own apartment but was nowhere near as successful as his twin brother Rory.

Being the older twin, Brandon had always felt like he should have accomplished more in life than Rory. Not that the few minutes separating their births really meant anything. Rory was just kinda charmed. Anything he did turned out well, where Brandon had to work hard for his successes. After years of school and some time working with a firm in Chicago, Brandon had been recruited to join Davis and Nill, Inc. As an architect, Brandon had thought he'd finally outshine his brother.

Rory had made big money off the web design company he'd started about the same time Brandon had left town for college. Brandon would be paying off student loans for years and Rory was talking about buying vacation homes in warm places.

Stop comparing yourself to him. He repeated the now familiar words. If he'd only listened to that bit of advice and not been so obsessed with outdoing his brother, he might still be married. Kathy had left him, claiming he was never around or there for her and that he put his job before her. It was hard to admit she did have a point, but when she married a former coworker a few months later, he didn't think it was all his fault.

Brandon showered quickly and rubbed the towel through his short hair. Maybe he should let it grow out a little. Set him apart from Rory. Brandon shook his head. He liked it shorter. *I don't have to change my life to accommodate Rory.*

Brandon wrapped his wet trunks in his towel and shoved them in his gym bag. As he walked out of the locker room, he saw the girl who'd joined him in the lap pool. She was tall and thin, her long arms made for powerful strokes. Her brown hair was wet and braided tightly, falling just between her shoulder blades.

She didn't seem to notice him, but he couldn't take his eyes off her. She was beautiful, and carried herself with confidence and assurance. She turned away from the counter where she'd been talking to the receptionist and met his eyes. Brandon took a slow breath, telling himself not to get involved, but as her eyes remained locked on his, interest flooded him.

Just before he could take a step forward to introduce himself, she frowned and looked away pointedly. She waved at the receptionist. "See you tomorrow, Janice."

Janice mumbled something without looking up. Brandon took the opportunity to watch the girl walk out the door then approached Janice at the desk. "How much for a membership?"

He hoped to see that beauty again.

Chapter Two

When she finished entering the reading scores for the last student, Shelly stood up and stretched. The second most enjoyable part of her day was over, and now she could swim and finish her leftovers from last night's takeout.

Shelly sighed. *How pathetic.*

The sting of Charlie's betrayal had subsided to a dull ache, but at times she had to work hard at keeping a positive attitude. She'd traveled to other countries to teach English and met Charlie in China the summer after she graduated from high school. He was one of the other teachers in the program. He'd charmed her right from the start, and they'd fallen in love.

A long distance relationship worked for them at first, while Shelly completed her degree in elementary education and Charlie finished his degree in engineering. He'd moved to Virginia near her to accept a job with a company helping to improve the living conditions of people in third world countries. He got involved in building low cost cement buildings that could withstand the hurricanes and also designing water purification plants for many countries in Africa.

She'd always admired his humanitarian work, and when he'd proposed a couple years ago, she'd accepted, knowing they could go make a difference in the world. But Charlie had been reluctant to set a date at first, and when she'd finally convinced him to commit to a date, she thought things would be smooth-sailing. Finding Charlie with another woman had soured her on men. She would take the time to heal and look at her options later. She loved children and wanted some of her own, but she had time, no matter what her parents thought.

Her students had been some of the most curious. Six and seven year olds were not known for their tact. Most of them were oblivious since they hadn't been with her last year and known about her upcoming wedding. A few had heard from the older students that Ms. Erikson was supposed to get married and move away. They had asked her innocent and actually sweet questions about why she was still there teaching, but how could she explain infidelity and betrayal to first graders?

She told them her plans had changed, and most of

8

them took that as answer enough. A couple of the more curious ones had offered advice.

"Just find a new guy to marry. There's lots out there."

She'd chuckled at their innocence at first, but as that same counsel was repeated by more and more people, she'd begun to resent it. At twenty-seven, she really wasn't in any rush to get married.

Shelly grabbed her purse and pulled her ID off her neck, tucking it into the pocket of her gym bag the moment she was out the school doors. Her blue Mustang purred as she started it up. Charlie had wanted her to switch to a smart car, but this was her dad's car and she'd always loved it. She pushed Charlie out of her thoughts once more and headed to the gym with the convertible top down. The pool called her name, and she couldn't wait to wash away her cares in the water.

Her lap lane was open, and the only other people in the pool area were using the sauna. Perfect. She adjusted her goggles and did her stretches before diving into the pool. The routine took over, and she glided through the laps. By the time she'd shifted to the breast stroke, she had been joined by another swimmer.

The swimmer was a man, she was sure of that. Too much skin to be female. Not wanting to be disturbed, she tried to ignore him, though she wouldn't be too upset if it was the same guy from yesterday. Shelly reminded herself how she'd tuned out distractions when she swam in high school competitions. How to be aware of the other swimmers' location enough to know how much to push herself but not be sidetracked.

She put on some speed, forcing the water to move out of her way. The man next to her kept pace right along with her. She enjoyed the competition. She hadn't swum next to anyone for a while, and she realized she missed it.

After switching to another stroke she did her customary ten laps and then finished off with a few lazy back strokes to cool down and catch her breath. Part of her wanted the guy in the pool to leave, and part of her wanted to talk to him. She up-righted herself to tread water. The man had his strong arms resting on the edge of the pool as he faced her. She smiled and moved toward him just a few feet.

He smiled in return and shook his head, making droplets of water splash. When he spoke, his deep voice carried across the pool without the crazy echoes most people would make. He was familiar enough with a pool to know how to talk in one.

"I haven't been out-swam for a long time."

Shelly raised an eyebrow and swam a few feet

closer. "You must not have been swimming in the right places."

He tilted his head to the side, showing his long, lean neck muscles. "Do you swim here daily?" he asked.

Shelly debated for a moment. Did she want him coming every day? Did she dare let this guy know anything about her? "Almost daily."

"I'm Brandon." He didn't offer his hand, and she was glad. She didn't want to come any nearer than she was.

"Shelly."

"It's been a pleasure to swim with you, Shelly." He put his hands on the edge of the pool, still not looking away from her and hefted himself backward onto the edge. He lifted one leg out, then the other, and stood up, smiling down on her. "I look forward to being soundly beaten again tomorrow." He turned and walked away leaving Shelly with a full view of his perfect physique. She blushed when he picked up his towel and turned to catch her staring. She gave a half-hearted wave and returned to her lazy back float.

Swimming with someone like him could be fun.

***

His heart rate had easily regulated itself after the

swim, but he still felt short of breath when he thought of Shelly. She hadn't seemed to notice him in the pool at first, but as he began his laps he knew when she sensed him. Her strokes had changed. She'd turned competitive on him, and he loved it. A powerful woman like that would be lots of fun to get to know. She didn't flirt at all, just seemed to be more focused on her swimming than on him.

Still, he'd caught her watching him after he'd exited the pool. She wasn't completely immune. It would be fun to see where this could go. Though he wasn't ready for anything serious, a little harmless flirting at the gym would be good for him. After Kathy left, he wasn't sure if he wanted to get involved again right away, but two years had passed, and he'd never opened his heart to the chance of anything. Shelly could be a good way to transition back into the dating world, build up a little confidence and get his mom and brother off his back.

As he walked out of the gym, he noticed the blue Mustang convertible he'd admired when he'd arrived. What he wouldn't give to have a chance to drive that. Someday he'd find a car like that for himself. He climbed into his Audi and headed to his brother's.

With his new job secure and a steady pay check coming in, Brandon no longer dreaded visiting Rory. He'd grown to love his niece, finding playtime with her actually enjoyable. Rory and his wife Michaela were loving and welcoming, but they were too full of questions and unhelpful dating advice. Rory had offered him a job as incentive to move back after Kathy left, but it had nothing to do with the architectural degree he'd worked so hard to earn. No, Brandon would do things on his own terms. It felt nice to be able to stand on his own without help from anyone.

Brandon took a slow breath and looked at the former church building sitting on a couple acres tucked behind rows of full trees. Rory wasn't flamboyant by any means, but his home was an amazing find. Brandon admired the progress that had been made. When Rory came to him for advice on how to remodel this old church into a home, without losing the uniqueness of the place, Brandon had been flattered. Brandon wanted to maintain the integrity of the chapel, including its hand carved woodwork and stained glass windows. They had collaborated on the project over the phone and through Skype calls. It was amazing to see what Rory had accomplished and where he'd taken Brandon's advice. His work on Rory's house had impressed Davis and Nill Architecture Inc. enough they'd tracked him down and made him an offer to work with them.

When they'd offered him the job, he'd debated

long and hard about if he wanted to return to his home town. It had taken a while to learn to accept that his strengths were different than Rory's. And coming back home would help him prove to himself he could stand on his own two feet and be in control of his life. Besides, his mom's health was declining and he didn't want to miss out on the last years of her life.

It would be good to be home. As Brandon reached the front door, Rory opened it and shook his hand.

"Come on in, Bran. Michaela made her breaded chicken and homemade rolls." Rory turned and Brandon followed him into the spacious home.

"I'm going to finish setting the table." Rory took a few steps toward the kitchen and dining room area tucked around the edge of what had been the chapel. He hollered up the stairs, "Jessica, come on down, sweetie."

Brandon looked up to see his niece at the top of the stairs that used to lead to the choir loft. The stain glass windows caught the evening sun, casting a colorful glow around her.

"Uncle Brandon!" Jessica shouted and ran down the stairs. Brandon braced himself and opened his arms to catch the excited eight-year-old. "I'm glad you came to our house." Jessica whispered when he hugged her. "You're more fun than Daddy."

Brandon couldn't help grinning, knowing he had one-upped his brother in this small way. "What game should we play after dinner this time? Do you have the same ones as Grandma?"

"No, but I have a new doll. I'll use her, and you can use the other ones."

He nodded along seriously, excited to know she liked his company and only slightly worried about playing dolls.

Rory peeked into the foyer. "Jessica, please bring your uncle to the dining room. Dinner's ready."

Jessica stopped jabbering immediately and a serious look crossed her face. "We'd better hurry. Mommy gets ornery when she's hungry." Brandon took a few steps, and Jessica spoke in a mock whisper. "She's hungry a lot. The baby inside her tummy must eat it all."

Brandon smiled and whispered back conspiratorially. "Then we'd better hurry so she doesn't eat our food."

Michaela raised an eyebrow at them as they entered the dining room. Brandon hoped she hadn't heard his teasing, not sure if he wanted his seven-months pregnant sister-in-law upset with him. She watched him as he pulled back the seat for his niece. Jessica grinned up at him as he pushed her chair in, and Brandon knew he'd scored a few more points as favorite uncle. Michaela smiled at him as he sat down and dished up a serving of chicken.

Brandon looked around the room, taking in the hand carved mahogany table that complimented the hardwood floors of the old chapel. The wide open spaces were broken up with little touches of Michaela's style and Brandon couldn't help approving of her choices.

"I love how you've kept the feel of the old building but have turned it into your own personal space. Not many people can do that."

Michaela smiled. "I had some great advice. Thank you for all your help on this project. It's been a dream of mine since I first saw one done in an article online."

"My pleasure. It's good to see the final product in person." He'd visited on occasion as the remodel had begun, but most of their interactions had been at his parent's house since his return to Virginia. This was the first time in the finished product.

"How are you enjoying your work?" Rory asked. "I heard you're working on the new library near your office."

"It's a great place to work. They do a lot to give back to the community."

"Now that you're settled, have you given any thought to Mom's request?" Rory asked.

Brandon frowned. That was a mild way of putting

16

their mother's obsession. "I'm always thinking of Mom's request, but until I meet the right girl, you'll have to be the one to give her grandkids."

Michaela patted her belly. "Yeah, we're working on it. But I know this great girl we could set you up with."

"I just got to town. Give me some time to look on my own first. I'm sure she's out there somewhere."

Rory and Michaela nodded and the conversation turned to safer topics, but Brandon couldn't help thinking of Shelly from the gym. He pushed that thought away, knowing he'd just met her. He shouldn't be thinking of kids with a practical stranger.

www.ingramcontent.com/pod-product-compliance
Lightning Source LLC
Chambersburg PA
CBHW070908180626
46817CB00003B/966